CHILDHOOD SWEETHEARTS

Passion, Love & Loyalty

A Novel

JACOB SPEARS

Good 2 Go Publishing

ISBN: 978-1-943686-74-2

Copyright ©2015

Published 2015 by Good2Go Publishing

7311 W. Glass Lane • Laveen, AZ 85339

www.good2gopublishing.com

twitter @good2gobooks

G2G@good2gopublishing.com

Facebook.com/good2gopublishing

ThirdLane Marketing: Brian James

Brian@good2gopublishing.com

Cover design: Davida Baldwin

Interior Layout: Mychea, Inc

Printed in the U.S.A.

"We're back, baby. Back to where we were before the money came."

"That's all I've ever wanted. I'm sure of that now."

ONE

Smooth walked out of the corner store gulping down the Gatorade he'd just bought, oblivious to the two white men making their way towards him.

"Hey there, Johnson," McBride said, slapping the bottle out of Smooth's hand.

"Shit!" the young man said as he attempted to run away, but was stopped by the larger of the two narcotics cops.

"We just want to talk to you," Briggs said, still holding on to Smooth's arm.

"Well, talk then, muthafucka. You don't have to hold me for that." He attempted to break free.

"What you got in your pockets? "McBride stuck his hand in the young man's pocket before he had a chance to answer.

"Jackpot!" McBride said, after pulling several small bags of marijuana from Smooth's pocket.

"Now, we can do this the easy way, or the hard way," Smooth remained quiet.

The two cops exchanged brief smiles.

"Just answer the questions for us and we'll pretend this encounter never took place," said Briggs.

"I'm listening."

"Where were you last night at 9:30?" McBride was doing the questioning.

"I was standing right there using that payphone," Smooth pointed.

"Did you see or hear anything unusual?"

"Sure did," Smooth answered, with a smile forming at the edges of his mouth.

"What'd you see?" McBride asked excitedly.

"Ain't see shit. I heard something though. That shit fucked me up."

"What did you hear, slut-head?" McBride was becoming fed up

with Smooth.

"I heard your mother asking me for phone sex." Smooth released the laughter he'd been holding.

Briggs hid his smile from his partner.

"I ain't know that bitch still had dick on her mind. But I should have known though, 'cause her son's a dickhead."

Still laughing, Smooth was handcuffed and thrown in the back of the car. Smooth was five months from his sixteenth birthday and he'd already been arrested nine times. Today would make the tenth.

* * *

"I got it!" China shouted, as she ran to the phone.

"Hello," she answered, nearly out of breath.

She listened while the recording stated that she had a collect call from a detention facility and the correct number to press to accept, however she knew exactly what to press. Thanks to Smooth, she was all too familiar with the juvenile detention center.

"What did you do this time?" China asked, just as the recording thanked her for accepting the call and ended.

"I ain't do shit. Why you always think a nigga did something?" Smooth snapped.

"Because you always do nigga, and you're not even smart enough to get away with it," China responded, holding her ground.

They both held the phones to their ears without saying anything for a few minutes. They got along because they were so much alike, but also so different from each other.

They were both stubborn, natural-born leaders. They were both extremely competitive and looked at second place as the first loser. Therefore, second place wasn't an option for either of them.

Of the two, China was the quiet one who believed trust was something to be earned and not given away freely. Because of that, she seldom allowed people to get close to her. But once you made your way into her heart, it was almost impossible to be pushed out.

At the age of 15, China could easily pass for a woman in her early 20's. She was the product of a Korean father and Trinidadian mother. Having acquired what seemed to be the best of both parents; China stood 5 feet, 7 inches and weighed 140 pounds. Her skin was the color of honey, with hair just a shade darker stopping just above an ass fat enough to make your wonder if it was real. And with breasts the size of baseballs, she knew she had it going on. Still, she never flaunted her body like other girls her age. Her mind was equally as developed as her body was.

That was one of the reasons Smooth was head over heels in love with her. Smooth was different from China. He was far more trusting. He allowed people to get close to him quickly and was just as quick to shut them out of his life if they violated his trust. It was obvious to all that Smooth would grow into a handsome young man. Girls a lot older than him always tried to gain his attention.

"Uhhh, uhhh," China cleared her throat.

Smooth knew from experience that that was her cue. She was ready to talk.

"Do you think you can get Roxy to come get me?" he asked.

Roxy was China's older sister who'd gotten Smooth out of lock-up on at least three different occasions.

"I'll ask. What *didn't* you do this time?"

He was used to her sarcasm.

"I did have a few bags of weed in my pocket."

China let out the breath she hadn't realized she was holding. In the past two years, Smooth had been arrested for everything from assault to grand theft auto. She was glad that all he had now was possession of marijuana.

"Is that the only charge you got?"

"That's the only one I told you, right?"

"Whatever!" said China smiling. She was also used to his sarcasm.

"Roxy will come get you."

For the remainder of the phone call, they talked about their plans for the future. That was something they often did.

"Roxy's here. We'll be there to get you soon," China said, just as the phone was about to hang up.

"Alright, I'm waiting," Smooth replied.

"Okay, don't drop the soap," China said, as she hung up the phone laughing. She knew he hated those words.

TWO

"This shit is hurting my finger," China allowed the scissors to fall from her hand and began rubbing her fingers.

"We almost finished girl. Pick that shit up and let's get through, so we can get up out of here."

"I can't, my fingers hurt," she whined.

"Ya fingers don't hurt when you counting money at the register buying up all that expensive shit."

"Whatever," China said, as she picked up the scissors again and began cutting up the big buds of weed.

She never told Smooth that her sister stole clothing for a living, which is where all of her new gear came from. He didn't know it, but China never spent any of the money he gave her for herself or the money he told her to "put up."

She saved because of the way Smooth spent. There was no way they could both spend recklessly and have anything left.

"Can't you sell another product?" she asked.

"Nope. Too much time. Weed ain't shit but a slap on the wrist."

"Then why not sell bigger quantities so we don't have to spend all this time breaking this shit up and I don't keep fucking up my nails?"

"The nigga won't sell me more than a pound at a time and this is the only way we can see any real money from this shit," Smooth told her.

"So we just got to find someone that will sell us more shit!"

"China, you act like we can just Google that shit. It ain't that fucking easy. Keep cutting."

She did as she was told. Not one to be easily sidetracked, China began thinking about where she could find a supplier who would be willing and able to sell her more weed.

Do you know where to cop one from?"

"What's up with you and the 20 questions?" Smooth asked, peering at China.

"Just answer the damn question, boy!"

"Maybe like five at a time. Shit, I don't know. Whatever we can get rid of."

"You need to think past this nickel and dime shit. We got to aim for the moon."

"We can think as big as we want; but reality is we don't got a connect, so we stuck with what we got."

China leaned over and smacked Smooth upside the head playfully.

"See, that's ya muthafuckin' problem right there. Stop worrying about the connect. Let me worry about that. You worry about the customer."

Smooth eyed her suspiciously. He knew China well enough to know that she was up to something.

"Who you been talking to?"

China fluttered her eyes innocently and answered, "Nobody!"

"Nobody my ass. Bitch, I should ..."

"Ya mama," China said, gripping the scissors by the handle firmly.

"You better watch your muthafuckin' mouth," Smooth warned, pointing at her from his seat.

"And you better watch yours, nigga!" China held her ground, never one to back down.

"Bring your ass here, girl," Smooth said, with a smile on his face.

China did as she was told.

"That better be the last time you pick up a weapon on me," he said, as he pulled her down on his lap.

"It will be, so long as you don't call me a bitch again."

"What about Queen Bitch?" Smooth teased.

"If I grab that scissors again, nigga, I will use it."

"I'm just teasing, boo," Smooth said, as he pulled her to him and placed a kiss on her lips.

"You know I love you, right?" he asked once their lips parted.

"I know what your mouth say."

"So you don't believe it then?"

China enjoyed toying with Smooth like she was currently doing. She knew that she was one of the few people in his life that he'd die for. She just liked hearing him say those three words.

"Of course I believe you, boy," she kissed his lips.

"What you got up your sleeves?" he wanted to know.

"Nothing!" she answered, as she got up from his lap and went to where she'd placed the scissors. She picked them up and began cutting again.

Smooth simply looked on.

"This is my last time doing this shit!" China completed.

"If you say so," Smooth replied.

* * *

The line at Club Heaven was stretched around the corner and it didn't seem to be moving. Still, everyone in line stayed in line. Everyone who was anyone in Miami would be present tonight. Several of the Miami Heat players were present, celebrating their championship win.

Occasionally, a bouncer would go down the line, pick five females of his liking, and admit them entrance to the club. Seeing him on his way down the line, Roxy tried her best to get noticed. While most of the girls in line touched their hair or wiggled their asses, she pretended to not notice what he was doing. He stopped in front of Roxy and her clique.

"You, you, and you!" he pointed.

Roxy, China, and Meka stepped out of line.

"Y'all go to the front," he ordered.

China watched as her sister and Meka began walking towards the entrance.

"Hello!" China barked, stopping them in their tracks.

The two females turned to look at her.

"What about them?" China pointed with her thumb at the other three females who'd come to the club with them.

Roxy had been coming to Club Heaven since it opened and had never gotten in. She wasn't about to turn down what might be her only chance.

"I'm going inside" was all she said. She then turned towards the entrance again, while Meka followed her.

China looked at the girls who were still in line and shrugged her shoulders as if to say, "I tried." She then took off after Roxy and Meka.

"Y'all ain't right!" China said, catching up.

"They would've done the same thing," Roxy explained to her younger sister. "And while we at it, let me explain a few things to you. You are not to leave my side. When I move, you move. The first sign of trouble, you make your way back to the car and wait for me. And if ma ever finds out about this, we're both dead. This is the first and last time I'm doing this, so don't even think about asking again."

China had not real desire to be at the club, so coming again was out of the questions. She was on a mission.

"None of the girls were asked for I.D. The bouncer who had them move to the front of the line simply snapped the passes onto their wrists and lifted the rope, allowing them to walk in.

"Now this is what I'm talking about," Meka screamed over the music, after looking around the plush club. It became obvious to them that they were in the presence of money.

Roxy pulled China's hand and headed towards the bar. Once the bartender returned with her order, she slid a glass in front of China who raised an eyebrow as if to ask, "What's this?"

"Water on the rocks, baby girl."

China smiled and picked up the glass.

"Now for your first lesson in spotting a baller," Roxy said, getting close enough to China so that she wouldn't have to scream.

"See him," Roxy was pointing at a young nigga that was obviously out of his element.

"He's what I call a *crawler*. That means a baby baller. He's not broke but he's also not balling. But to act the part, he'll go broke pretending to be a baller."

China listened to her sister's philosophy. Pointing again, Roxy said, "He's a broker." Clearly he's not broke." This was evident by the man's clothes and jewelry. He's a legit businessman who likes to have fun in bed. He'll make a deal with any girl he leaves with tonight."

Roxy took a sip of her drink and then continued.

"Let's go to the pleaser. He's known as a pleaser because he has no style or class about himself. Everything he acquires is done so to please the people around him. His clothes, cars, jewels, and even his woman are all about making the next man notice him. All his money comes from the dope game. He's more than likely ..."

China had heard all she needed. The pleaser was her man. Roxy was under the impression that China wanted to come to Club Heaven to celebrate her birthday with her. Truth is that China had heard that this was where she needed to be if she was trying to find a baller. That often translated to hustler. So here she was.

"She watched the pleaser, waiting for a chance to speak to him. She knew that as long as she was at her sister's side, she wouldn't be allowed to talk to pleaser or any other man.

Almost on cue, Mellow walked up from behind.

"Happy birthday," he whispered into Roxy's ear.

She pretended not to see her ex-boyfriend, but her smile betrayed her. She was happy to see him and even happier that he remembered her birthday.

"Hey Mellow," she feigned indifference.

"What are you doing in here dressed like that?" he turned his attention to China.

"I brought her here," Roxy answered.

Mellow gave Roxy an evil look.

"I'll be right back. I got to use the restroom," China excused herself.

Walking in the general direction of the restrooms, China scanned the club, hoping to find the pleaser, feeling confident that he was available to talk.

He was standing several feet away from the ladies room entrance, talking to a pretty dark-skinned female who was wearing a tight, white mini dress that showed off her curves. China impatiently watched them whisper back and forth to each other.

Finally, she'd had enough. She purposely bumped into him as she walked by. With fire in his eyes, the pleaser turned, ready for a confrontation.

"Oh, I'm sorry," China apologized, ignoring the dirty look she was getting from the woman in the tight dress.

"Nah, you good," the pleaser said, as he smiled at the young female standing in front of him.

"S'cuse me," China extended her hand to the pleaser, who gladly accepted it.

She slipped the paper in his palm, smiled, and walked off. She stole a glance over her shoulders as she walked off. Just as she thought, he was staring at her ass.

When she returned to the bar, Mellow had his arms around Roxy's waist and they were both smiling.

"Are you enjoying yourself?" China asked, reclaiming her seat.

"Not really," answered Roxy.

"Me neither." Now that she'd accomplished what she'd come to do, China was ready to leave.

"Go find Meka so that we can go."

THREE

Smooth walked into the house unannounced. Anytime Ms. Jenkins' car wasn't in the driveway, he'd walk right in.

"My connect just got snatched up," he told China.

"That's too bad for him."

"Him? Shit, what about us? We fucked!"

"Never that. That's what I wanted to talk to you about," China said as she patted the seat next to her on the couch.

"Listen, I know you're not going to like what I'm about to tell you and I know it'll be hard for you, but try to keep an open mind. I did what I did for us."

Smooth wasn't liking what he was hearing. "Talk," he said through clenched teeth.

China got up from next to him and began speaking slowly.

"Do you remember the night I went out with Roxy for her birthday?"

Smooth nodded.

"Well, we went to Heaven and I met someone. His name is Boss and ..."

"Bitch," Smooth said, barely audibly.

Before he knew it, China's hand was connecting with the left side of his face.

"Smooth shot to his feet and drew back to punch China, but stopped just as he saw Ms. Jenkins' car pull into the driveway.

"This ain't over," he warned.

"You damn right it ain't nigga. I can't believe you was about to hit me. I got you muthafucka!" China stared Smooth down.

"About to, bitch? You did hit me!"

"Ya mama. Ya mama. Ya mama," China took a step closer to him every time she spoke.

"Hi Ga Ga," Smooth said, acknowledging China's mom.

"Hey Smooth. How are you?"

"I'm fine and you?"

"Tired. What y'all two in here going at each other about?" Ga Ga asked the two teenagers in front of her.

"Nothing!" they answered in unison.

She eyed them both suspiciously.

"Okay, if anyone calls for me, take a message. I'm going to get some rest." With that, she headed to her bedroom.

China stood in front of Smooth with her hands on her hips, waiting for round two.

"I'm out of here, man," Smooth said, as he attempted to get up, but was pushed back down.

"I called you over here to tell you something, and before you leave you will hear me out."

"Hurry up. Say what you gotta say."

"Don't rush me, nigga," China responded, full of attitude.

"I don't know why I put up with your shit!"

"Because you love me. Now shut up and listen."

All he could do was smile. She was right.

"Like I was saying, I met a nigga that goes by the name of Boss. I gave him my number and we've talked a few times. He thinks my name is Nakia and I'm 22. Besides what I've just told you, he doesn't know anything else."

"Where is all of this shit going?" Smooth asked.

"If you be quiet, you'll find out. Baby, I know you're upset, but please just hear me out. If you're still upset when I get through, then I'll accept whatever you send my way. Deal?"

"We needed to find a connect so that we can start making some money. That's where this nigga Boss comes in. He's got the whole of Opa-Locka on lock. The warehouses belong to him, too. I figured I'd be doing us a lot of good if I can cop from him."

How do you know he'd sell to you?"

"I don't know; but if he doesn't, then we'll just rob his ass!" China said without a trace of a smile.

"First of all, I'm not talking no robbing shit. I'm talking about a connect. If he won't give us what we need, we'll take it. It's that simple."

"You need to find out everything you can and quickly. I only got a quarter pound left, and then we're through."

"Let me take care of this. As a matter of fact, I'll call him right now," China dialed Boss' number, and then took a seat next to Smooth while putting her phone on speaker. After two rings, he picked up.

"Who dis?"

"It's me, Boss."

"Me who?"

"You forgot about me that quickly, huh?"

"Never that! What's up, NAKIA?" Boss emphasized her name.

"You tell me what's up! I was hoping I'd be able to see you."

"When you want to see me?" he asked.

"I'm supposed to meet my girls in an hour; but depending on where you are, I might be able to swing by before then."

"Do you know where the warehouses are on 22nd, just off 151st?"

"I'm sure my lil' brother knows," China lied, but looking for a reason to bring along Smooth.

"Okay, my car is in front of the second one on the right."

"How will I know it's your car?"

"Trust me, you'll know!"

With that, they both hung up the phone.

* * *

Roxy was right, China thought, as Smooth parked behind the CLS55 Mercedes Benz. Everything about the car screamed, "Look at me."

She picked up her phone and dialed Boss' number.

"I'm outside," she said, after the man answered.

Boss exited the warehouse wearing what looked like a million dollars' worth of jewelry.

"What a clown," China mumbled while exiting the car.

"DAMN, NAKIA! I knew you had it going on, but not like this!" Boss said, as he spun her around slowly while licking his lips.

Just the sight of Boss with his hands on China made Smooth's grip on the steering wheel tighten.

"Can we get out of the sun?" China asked, hoping to get a look inside.

"For sho!" Boss said, as he took her by the hand and led the way.

Once inside his office, Boss took a seat behind his desk and put his feet up.

"So, Boss, tell me about yourself."

That was all he needed her to say.

"I'm like my name. I'm the boss around here. I run all this and a lot more. I got everything a nigga can want except a female good enough to call wifey. I need me a down-ass bitch. You think you got what it takes to be my down-ass bitch?"

At that moment, China wanted to reach across the desk and smack the shit out of the Mr. T wannabe sitting in front of her who wouldn't stop licking his lips. But she resisted the urge rising within her.

"It depends," she answered instead.

"On?"

"What's required of your down-ass bitch."

That was a first for Boss. Every other female he'd ever asked that question said yes without so much as a second thought.

"Where you see yourself five years from now?" he asked.

China thought for a second and then answered the questions as if it were Smooth she was talking to. She told Boss exactly where she planned on being at 27.

After she'd finished, Boss smiled.

"Brains and beauty. That's a lethal combo."

China only smiled.

"That all sounds good, but it takes a lot of money to start some shit like that. Where do you plan on getting that type of money?"

"I got a lot of time. I'll get it. Trust me, I'll get it."

Boss stayed quiet but secretly admired China's determination.

"If you need my help, let me know."

For the next 15 minutes, the two talked about Boss' life. China only answered the questions he asked her, volunteering as little information as possible and making sure to remember every lie she told him.

Just as he was instructed, Smooth dialed China's number 25 minutes after she'd left the car.

"I got to get going," she told Boss, once she hung up.

He jumped to his feet and ran to her side of the desk.

"When am I going to spend some real time with you?" boss asked, holding both of China's hands.

"Let's not rush things." She knew exactly what he was referring to.

With that, she gave him a kiss on the check, turned around, and walked out.

* * *

Smooth was extremely moody. It had been two weeks since he ran out of weed and he was still no closer to finding a connect. Not that he wasn't trying, he was. His mood only grew darker every time a customer approached him.

He was sitting in his usual spot listening to the niggas in his crew talk shit to each other. Smooth was an excellent reader but he was even better with numbers, despite dropping out of school in the seventh grade. The fact that he no longer attended school was a sore spot in his and China's relationship. He wished every nigga had a girl like China. To him, there was nothing better. He'd been with her since they were both 12, and the closest he'd ever gotten to sex with her was some heaving foreplay that involved oral sex on both parts. And that was only one time. The fact that they never had sexual intercourse didn't take away from the way Smooth felt about her. If anything, it actually added to it. China was his for life. At least that's how he felt

"So you telling me that Lil' Wayne is worth more than Jay Z?" Banga asked Bobby.

"You muthafucka right he is!"

"Tell me how you came to that conclusion?"

"Nigga, I ain't they fuckin' accountants! I just know."

"You stupid as fuck!" Banga said.

Smooth was used to his two friends going at it with each other, but he wasn't in the mood for it at the moment.

"Both you niggas stupid. Shut that shit up, man!" he barked at both Bobby and Banga.

The two boys fell silent.

"We got some shit coming up and y'all want to do is argue over which rapper got more paper. Fuck them niggas! Let's focus on getting our own shit!"

Still silence.

Smooth pulled a $20 from his pocket and handed it to Neko, the baby of the crew.

"Go get some drinks," he ordered.

"Neko got on his bicycle and rode off.

"Listen up," Smooth addressed everyone remaining. "I'm planning a nice come-up for us. We need ..."

Smooth and his crew turned in the direction of the car horn. He walked over to China.

"What's up?" he asked, leaning against the car.

"Boss just gave me keys to his crib. I got security codes and everything. He said he wants to see me there when he gets there tonight. I told him that I'd definitely be there."

Smooth nodded his head.

"I will be there, right?" China asked, placing her hand on Smooth's hand.

"Yeah, we'll be there," he answered.

"Who are you planning on bringing with you?" she wanted to know.

Smooth looked over his shoulder as he spoke, prompting China to also look.

"I'm only bringing Head and Mo."

"Okay," China nodded in agreement. "Here's everything you'll need." China handed over the key she had along with the codes and directions.

FOUR

Smooth had spent his last bit of money on the two guns, one of which he held tightly in his grip. The other was sitting at the bottom of China's handbag. Smooth checked his watch again to make sure they were on schedule. He'd told China that they'd be there at 8:00.

None of the three young niggas in the truck did drugs, so they listened to the music that emanated from the speakers. The boys bobbed their heads as the rapper rapped about the thrill he got from robbing.

"Over there," Smooth pointed, directing Mo, who was driving the stolen car they were in, to go where the residents of the private community gained entrance.

"Don't let the window down," Smooth ordered. "Crack the door open and enter the code."

Mo did as he was told and then watched as the gate slowly opened.

"Turn there," Smooth continued, giving him directions.

After making a series of turns, they finally found the house they were looking for. The house wasn't a mansion, but it was far bigger than any house any of the three boys had stepped in before or even seen, for that matter.

"Wait a minute!" Smooth got out and rang the doorbell repeatedly until he was convinced there was no one at the house. He pulled the keys out and opened the door.

Smooth found the keypad on the wall a few feet away from the door and punched in the security code. The beeping stopped just as he expected. He went back outside.

"China should be calling me any minute now. When she does, that means that they're at the gate. When you get a call from me, head back here, and wait until we come out," he instructed Mo.

Head got out of the truck and together he and Smooth walked through the front door.

"This nigga ballin'," Head said.

"Yeah, I know," Smooth said, as he looked around admiring his surroundings.

At last, his phone rang. It was China.

"They're at the gate. Kill the lights."

The two boys took their positions, one behind the door and one behind the couch. They waited for the door to open. When Boss opened the door, he sensed something wasn't quite right, but he couldn't place his finger on it. China sensed that he'd picked up on something and turned toward him. Placing a hand on his crotch, she whispered to him, "Are you read to have some fun?"

Boss kicked the door closed without as much as a look over his shoulders.

"You know I am. You made me wait long enough," he said.

"Me too," Smooth said, as he placed the gun to the back of Boss' head.

"Put your hands up, muthafucka!"

Boss did as he was told.

"Hit the light."

Head got up from his hiding spot and hit the light switch.

"We ain't got all day, nigga, and the more questions I ask the less chance you have of walking away alive. Start talking."

Boss couldn't believe the two young niggas in his house.

"Y'all lil' niggas know who the fuck I am?" he snapped, turning to look at Smooth, who had backed up but was still pointing the gun at this head.

"I'm telling you Boss, don't make me do it," Smooth was trying his hardest to sound convincing but failing miserably. He hadn't expected Boss to be this defiant.

Because his eyes were glued to Smooth, Boss never saw China pull a gun from her handbag.

"Of course, he knows who you are. I told him all about you."

Boss turned to see China pointing a gun at him; but unlike Smooth, her hands were steady.

"Head, come here," she ordered. "Reach in my bag and get the cuffs."

Head pulled out a set of handcuffs.

"Cuff his hands behind his back."

Head approached Boss carefully, instructing him to turn around. In one swift motion, Boss spun around and grabbed Head, placing him in a headlock. He flipped open the small knife attached to his key ring and placed it at Head's throat.

"Now what?" he smiled.

Without warning, China squeezed the trigger twice, hitting Head in the chest. The boy was dead before his body hit the floor.

"Let's try this again," China said as she stared at Boss. "Put the cuffs on him, Smooth."

Smooth swung the butt of his gun and connected it with the back of Boss' head.

When Boss finally opened his eyes, his hands were locked behind his back.

"Get up," China instructed, as she kicked him in the ass. "I'm going to ask you only one time. Where should I look in this house for money and jewelry?"

Not wanting to take any chances with the woman in front of him, Boss gave it all up. Smooth listened until he was finished and then began his search. He re-entered the room carrying a large duffle bag.

"Take him to the car. His car," China instructed, clearly running the show now.

Smooth helped him to his feet and picked up the keys. China headed into the garage as the two men headed outside.

Smooth opened the door to the car and made Boss lay flat on the backseat. China walked back into the house carrying a plastic container of gasoline. Carefully, she poured gas throughout the house, with a large emphasis on Head's body. Walking out the front door, she threw the lit book of matches over her head.

"Drive to the warehouses," she instructed Mo, before getting in Boss' car with Smooth.

"You drive. I'll keep my eyes on him."

* * *

The drive to the warehouse was a long one for both Smooth and China.

Smooth thought about Head the entire time and wished that China hadn't killed him. Even though his friend was dead, Smooth admitted to himself that he also might have been dead had it not been for China's actions. Who knows what Boss had planned. He looked over at her and smiled.

China wished they'd hurry up and get there. It would be hard to explain what a man was doing cuffed in the back seat if they were to get pulled over.

What seemed like an eternity was actually only 20 minutes after they'd left Boss' house. They arrived at the warehouse safely.

"You better pray we didn't come here for nothing," China said before exiting the car. It was almost 9:00 p.m. and there was no activity going on around any of the warehouses.

"Let's go, nigga," Smooth said, as he grabbed Boss' arm, helped him out of the car, and walked him to the door. Once the door was opened, Boss realized what was wrong when he opened the door to his house. The alarm never beeped.

"Turn it off," Smooth said.

"Where is it?" he asked, once the alarm was quieted.

Boss pointed at the far wall. Together they all walked over.

"Where?" Smooth asked.

"Hand me the remote, right there," Boss instructed, as had decided to fully cooperate. He pressed a series of buttons on the remote and they watched as the walls opened up, revealing thousands of pounds of marijuana.

China and Smooth both smiled. Boss closed his eyes and prayed for the day when he'd be able to kill both of them.

"Bring the truck and hurry," Smooth said into the phone to Mo.

Smooth walked over to the wall and picked up a bale of the weed. What he was holding felt as if it weighed about 30 pounds. There were probably 100 to 150 that same size stacked up against the wall.

Mo arrived and pulled the truck inside, just as Smooth ordered him. Together, the two boys and China loaded up the truck.

"Oh, before I forget," China said, as she picked up a rag and ran outside. "I had to wipe down the car." She smiled at Smooth. "And get this."

"Bitch, I'm going to kill you," Boss spat at China.

"Not before I kill you," she responded, as she raised her gun.

"China, no!" Smooth yelled at her. "Let me."

"She hates to be called a bitch," Smooth said as he raised his gun and placed it toward Boss' head. Without another word, he squeezed the trigger.

The sight of the blood oozing from the man's head, along with the vacant look in his eyes, was too much for Mo. He emptied the contents of his stomach onto the floor of the warehouse.

"What the fuck is wrong with you?" Smooth snapped.

"We wasn't supposed to kill nobody," he cried.

China couldn't believe what she was hearing.

"Let's get out of here, Smooth. You drive."

He went around and got into the driver's seat. China slowly stepped up into the cab and looked back at Mo.

"Thanks for your help," she said, as she squeezed the trigger until there were no bullets left.

"Take me home," she said to Smooth.

"What now?" he asked, as he pulled up in front of her house.

"My job was to get us a connect. Your job was to get rid of the work. I got us the work; now it's on you."

"I'll take care of it."

"I know you will. Give me that bag," she requested, as she pointed to the bag holding the money and jewelry they'd taken from Boss' house.

Smooth handed her the bag.

"Give me that gun, too. I'll get rid of them."

After handing the gun to her, Smooth put the truck in drive.

"I love you, China," he said.

"I love you more, Smooth. Please be careful."

"I will be."

With that, he drove off.

FIVE

Four months had passed since that which the media called "the warehouse murders." Four months and everyone, including the police, was still completely clueless as to who was responsible. Rumor had it that the Jamaicans had ordered the hit on Boss because he was interfering with their profits. The young boy killed just happened to be in the wrong place at the wrong time. Another rumor had it that Boss had robbed some Mexicans out of Arizona awhile back, and they'd finally caught up with him, partly in thanks to the dead boy. There were many rumors, all of which pleased Smooth because they were all far from the truth. Just three days after his 16th birthday, Smooth sat in the driver's seat of a new cherry red BMW M3—his birthday present from China.

Roxy had received a safety deposit box for China to store the jewels that they'd taken from Boss. They still didn't know how much they were worth. Smooth and China both agreed that the weed should be moved as quickly as possible. They placed each pound at $300. With them having 147 bales at 30 pounds a bale, they were looking at a street value of $1.3 million. Combined with the cash they'd also stolen, they were sitting comfortably on more than $2 million. Yet no one had a clue. The car was the only thing they'd purchased. China was still spending the few thousand dollars she saved from her and Smooth's nickel-and-dime days.

Smooth turned his head and spoke to the young nigga in the passenger seat.

Brazen was the often mistaken for a pretty boy due to his light skin and neat braids.

"You think these niggas official?" Smooth asked.

"I know they are nigga. You just paranoid as fuck. We good, yo!"

Brazen was 19 and fresh on the scene from Brooklyn, New York. His reason for moving to Miami was that he'd just graduated from high school and wanted a life where it didn't snow. That's what he told everyone. Smooth knew better, thanks to China.

Brazen's real name was Brandon Valasquez. He fled from Brooklyn because of his role in a dismantled drug ring. According to the Kings County D.A. Office, Brazen was a top-ranking figure in what he called the largest drug ring he'd seen in his career.

The ring reportedly trafficked hundreds of pounds of marijuana a week, along with dozens of kilos of cocaine and other dugs along the East coast. After learning that bit of information, Smooth thought that the D.A. must have had a short career. He knew of individuals that moved more work than that. At least he knew one.

"I ain't paranoid by a long shot. I'm just careful."

"Come on," Brazen said, getting out of the car, as the other car entered the parking lot.

"Yo, Sleep, what's good, my nigga?" Brazen greeted the first of the two men as they approached.

"Life, nigga. What's good on your end?"

"Everything. What's the deal, Meeks?" Brazen greeted the other dude.

"Maintaining ... maintaining." Meeks said, nodding his head.

"Let's do this, niggas," Sleep said, shifting his attention to Smooth.

Smooth's hands were in his pockets. His right hand gripped tightly to his pistol.

"What you got for us?" Sleep asked.

"What you got for me?" Smooth returned the question.

Sleep smiled and nodded his approval. He went back to his car and pulled a tote bag from the backseat.

"It's all there," Sleep said, as he tossed the bag to Smooth, who caught it with his left hand.

After looking in the bag, Smooth picked up his phone and dialed a number.

"Come on," he said, before hanging up.

"I'm assuming that's the work you just called for," Sleep said to Smooth.

Smooth shook his head.

Two minutes later, China pulled into the parking lot and headed over to where the four men were waiting. Smooth walked to the trunk of the car and tapped on it. When it opened, he pulled out the duffle bag and replaced it with the tote bag. He tapped the trunk again and watched as the car pulled off.

Brazen walked over to help Smooth with the bag.

After placing the bag in the trunk of the car, Sleep opened it so that he and Meeks could take a look inside.

Satisfied, they nodded to Smooth and Brazen.

"We'll be in touch," Sleep said to Smooth, just before he got in the car.

"Do that," Smooth responded.

* * *

Smooth pulled up to China's house and hit the horn.

"Hey handsome," she said, leaning over the driver's side after entering the car. She gave him a kiss.

"Hi beautiful. How's Ga Ga?"

"She's good. Sleeping as usual. She's going to be pissed when I tell her I'm moving out."

"That's what I wanted to talk to you about," Smooth said, as he pulled China onto his side of the car.

"What's up?" she asked skeptically.

"I think we should hold up on moving in together."

"Why? This was your idea all along."

"Brazen lined up a few deals for us that's gonna take us out of town if all goes well. We'll be going out of town a lot. I don't want to be worried about you while I'm taking care of business," he told her.

"I can take care of myself, boy."

"Yeah, I know, but it'll still be distracting for me."

Even though it wasn't what she wanted to hear, she knew he was right and agreed with him.

"So when are we going to get our own place?" China asked.

"Soon." China shook her head.

"What?"

"I need a more specific date than that."

"I don't know what else to tell you, boo."

"You need to come up with something and quick."

"I haven't told Brazen how much shit we got. What I'll do is tell him and see how long he thinks it'll take for us to move it. Whatever he tells me, then we'll move."

China was shaking her head once more.

"What's wrong now?" Smooth asked her, exhaling loudly.

"Don't give me your lil' funky-ass attitude, boy," China answered with an attitude of her own. "I just think it's a bad idea for you to tell Brazen what we got. I'll just be patient."

"You will?" Smooth replied, not expecting it be so easy.

"Yeah, I'll wait."

"That's my girl."

Smooth pulled her face to his and began kissing her as he slid his hand in her pants. China's wet warmness always made Smooth wonder what it would feel like to finally be inside of her.

"Stop before Ga Ga sees us," China warned.

Smooth never pressured China for sex. He knew exactly when she'd be ready. He'd heard her tell Roxy that she'd do it for her 16th birthday. He'd been waiting for years, so two more months wouldn't hurt he reasoned. And if he wanted it before then, he knew of several females that were more than willing to please him. He preferred to wait. He and China would lose their virginity at the same time to each other.

He removed his hand from her pants.

"What if I can help you get rid of it?" she asked.

"Nope," Smooth shook his head.

"What about us getting our own place, and I'll stay here when you go out of town? That way I can take care of you whenever you get back."

Again, he began shaking his head.

"Just think about it, please," China purred.

"Okay, I will."

"Let's go inside," she instructed.

Hand in hand, the two young lovers entered the house.

"Well, if it isn't Romeo and Juliet," Ga Ga teased, as she came out of the kitchen.

"What's up Ga Ga?" Smooth said, while wrapping his arms around her.

"My blood pressure. I'm so tired of working hard and still not getting anywhere. That's why it's important for y'all to get an education. In the world today, you got to have an education. You need to be smart about a lot of things and real smart about everything else. Your education is the only thing that can't be taken away from you. That's why I'll continue to work my fingers to the bone. My babies are going to college."

China, who was sitting on the couch flipping through the latest edition of *Don Diva* magazine, seemed to sink a little deeper after hearing her mother's words. She had no plans of going to college.

"You don't need to do that, Ga Ga," China told her mother.

"Child, hush! I'm going back to bed. Y'all be good."

With that, Ga Ga left them alone.

* * *

After wrapping up a deal in which he sold 200 pounds to a Haitian from the northwest section of Miami, Smooth decided to pick up an apartment guide. China's 16th birthday was only a month away and he wanted it to be the best day of her life. He decided to get their own place, just as they'd planned all along.

One of the places that caught this eye was located in Aventura. It had all of the amenities he and China could possibly ever want and then some. He called the number and arranged to see the place. The leasing agent said that she'd be available any time and that he could come by any time before four.

Smooth thanked her and hung up the phone. He was eager to see the place, but before could do that, he called up China to let her know he was on his way over.

"What's up Monica?" Smooth greeted the female exiting China's house, just as he arrived.

"Ain't nuttin'" she said, biting her bottom lip as she walked past him.

Monica and China had been best friends since the first grade and did practically everything together. She was the one who China had called when she first got her period. To all who could see, their bond was unbreakable.

"What my girl doing?" he asked, ignoring what she'd just done.

"Go find out," she answered, as she walked away adding some twist to her hips.

Smooth contemplated telling China about Monica's actions but decided against it. Ever since he'd been driving his M3, the attention he'd been getting from the opposite sex increased ten-fold, including from Monica. Periodically, she'd call him just to make small talk. Initially, Smooth hadn't thought anything of it, until her intentions became clear. He changed his number, but several hours later Monica would have his new one. He changed his number two more times; however, Monica got those new numbers, so he gave up.

"Hi handsome," China greeted him, as he walked through the door.

"Hey beautiful," Smooth said as he pulled her into his arms.

"How's your day going so far?" she asked.

"It's going good. I just need some time to take care of a few things."

"How much?" China asked.

"I'm not sure. I got something I need to take care of. I'll see you when I get back."

"Okay."

Back in his car, Smooth thought about Monica. She was his girlfriend's best friend, so why was she coming on to him so strongly. Even though she was able to give China a run for her in the beauty department, surely she didn't think he'd leave his girl for her or even risk it. He wondered if China put her up to it. But he quickly pushed the thought aside. If China even though Monica was trying to make a move on him, he thought, she'd probably kill her.

Smooth was the only person alive who'd seen that treacherous side of China.

"Maybe I should put Brazen on her," he said to himself.

He dialed his number.

"You busy tonight?" he asked.

"Why, what's the deal?" Brazen responded.

"My girl and I are going out and she wants to bring Monica along. I'm going to need someone to keep either me or Monica company.

"That the slanted-eye, red-bone beauty?"

"That's her," Smooth replied.

"I'm ya man, most def!"

After confirming with Brazen, Smooth called to inform China of his plans. She agreed and said that she'd call her friend.

* * *

Smooth made it to the leasing office a few minutes before 3:00 and was greeted warmly by a brown-skinned sister with long, neat dreads pulled back into a ponytail.

"Hi, my name is Miranda Burkley. How can I help you today?"

"Hi Ms. Burkley, my name's Donavan Johnson. I believe I spoke with you earlier about a place in Aventura."

"Oh yeah, come this way."

Miranda guided Smooth to her office where she offered him several different refreshments, all of which he politely declined.

She poured herself a drink from behind her desk.

After being as specific as possible, Smooth was asked to follow Ms. Burkley to another room.

He watched as the lights were lowered and the image from the projector covered the wall.

"If you see anything that catches your interest, let me know; and if you'd like, we can go and take a look at it. This way saves us time and money."

Smooth watched as the cameraman walked the full length of the back and front yards, and then toured the inside.

The place was beautiful but not what he wanted.

Ms. Burkley moved on to the next.

After several places, Smooth finally came across one he thought was perfect for him and China.

It was located on the 16th floor of a 25-story high rise that was right in the heart of Aventura. Everything about the place screamed class and sophistication.

"That one," Smooth said.

Ms. Burkley took down the address and then turned the lights back on.

"When would you like to see it?" she asked.

"I just did."

"It's much nicer in person."

"I'm sure it is," Smooth answered. "Let's get the paperwork completed."

"Don't you want to know how much your rent will be?"

"I never asked because it doesn't matter."

"This way," Ms. Burkley said, as she guided Smooth back to her office, concealing the smile on her face. She was impressed.

"We're going to need your first and last months' rent, security deposit, and membership fees in advance," she informed him.

After counting the money she'd received from Smooth, Ms. Burkley had him sign some papers and then handed him his keys.

"Thank you for your business, Mr. Johnson. And if there's anything I can do for you, please let me know."

"I'll remember that. Thank you."

Smooth turned and headed for the door.

"Oh, Mr. Johnson," Ms. Burkley called out, as she approached him.

"Yes," Smooth turned.

"Just one more thing."

"What's that?"

"A young black man driving an expensive car with a pocket full of money screams drug dealer."

Ms. Burkley watched as Smooth's shoulders sagged, confirming what she already knew.

"No need to worry, your secret is safe with me. But I do have some suggestions for you."

"I'm listening."

"Rather than walking around with your packets bulging out from the illegal money you're making, why not go get yourself a couple credit cards, even if they're pre-paid," she suggested.

Smooth nodded his head.

"And," Ms. Burkley continued, "why not drive a more common car?"

Smooth nodded again.

"How many red M3s do you think you'll see between here and your next destination? Just something for you to think about. You got my number if you need me," she said turning away and dismissing Smooth.

SIX

Smooth went over his list for the umpteenth time. He wanted to make sure everything was just right. Today was China's birthday and he wanted nothing left to chance. He called the car dealer to check up on the Range Rover he'd purchased for her and was told that the vehicle was ready to be picked up. With that out of the way, he grabbed his keys and headed over to the jewelry store. Everything was going well. He decided to place a call to China.

"Hey birthday girl," Smooth said, when she picked up.

"Hi, baby, where are you?"

"I'm at the store getting something special for you."

"What'd you get me?" she asked excitedly.

"Why you even asking when you know I'm not going to tell you."

"Can't blame a girl for trying," China said coolly.

"Not at all. What time does the party start?"

"Ga Ga wants everyone gone by 11:30 p.m., so we'll start partying around 6:00 ... five and a half hours to celebrate my sweet 16. That's not fair."

"I'm surprised she's letting you have a party at her house at all!"

"I know, right," China said giggling.

"What color are you wearing tonight?" Smooth asked.

"My favorite, of course."

That's what Smooth was hoping to hear.

"I got a few more things I need to take care of. I'll talk to you later."

"Okay baby, be careful out there. I love you."

"Always. I love you, too."

* * *

Smooth prepared himself for the smell of the pet shop and then walked in. The puppies he was interested in were located at the very back of the store. Smooth stood over the playpen that housed the animals. China had always wanted a pit bull but her mother wouldn't allow it, claiming that the dogs were illegal in Dade County. The truth was that Ga Ga was terrified of the dogs. She'd been attacked by one when she was a teenager and had never gotten over the fear the dog had placed in her. She offered China the compromise of another kind of dog, but China had refused them all.

As Smooth looked at the puppies, he tried imagining which one his girl would be most happy with. They were all pretty so that wasn't an issue. He grabbed one of the ones jumping about by the head and shook it. When he let go, the puppy ran away from him. Smooth did the same thing to another puppy. This time when he let go, the dog only looked at him. He did it again, and the dog whimpered to the back of the pen beside the first. There was one that Smooth had purposely ignored because of its size. It was the smallest one. He moved away from the two puppies and came up to him and held out his hand to shake his head just as he'd done the other two. Only this time he stopped in mid-air. The dog was growling and showing his teeth. Smooth smiled. He found the one he was looking for. He instructed the sales associate to have the puppy fully groomed after picking up everything he thought the dog would need. Smooth paid and told the associate he'd be back before they closed at the end of the day.

His next stop was to the jeweler he'd hired to make a one-of-a-kind locket that would hold two pictures inside of him and China. The first picture would be the most recent picture he and China had taken together. And the other picture would be the very first picture they had taken together. It was a picture that was sure to make China cry. It was their first-grade class photo, and they were standing next to each other. Rather than looking at the camera, Smooth was standing next to China looking at her. The jeweler apologized for the delay and promised to have it ready in less than an hour.

With some time to kill, Smooth walked through the mall to see if there was anything he wanted to buy. His mind was on several different things as he walked. Besides China, Smooth thought about what he'd do once all of the weed was gone. He managed to get rid of anywhere from 400 to 500 pounds every week. He was doing well but was eager to move the rest of it, which was more than 2,000 pounds.

Brazen was a big help, but with each sale that Brazen lined up, Smooth's profits were shortened. Smooth constantly reminded himself that it was all profit.

Seeing a pair of Nike Air Max's that coordinated with the colors that China would be wearing, Smooth had the sales person bring him a pair in his size as well as a pair for China.

After paying with his credit card, he headed back to the jeweler.

* * *

"What's up, Foxy Roxy?" Smooth greeted the only female he'd ever looked at as an older sister.

"Heyyyy," Roxy replied, taking a sip of whatever it was she was drinking.

"Where's the birthday girl?" he asked.

Roxy tilted her head towards the house.

"Come here, boy," Roxy stopped him. "We need to talk."

"Yeah, we do," he turned around.

"What's on your mind?" she asked.

"You first."

"Alright. Today is China's 16th birthday."

"Nah, for real?" Smooth replied sarcastically.

Roxy smacked him in the head playfully.

Besides China, the woman in front of him was the only other person that put their hands on him and got away with it.

"Shut up. I'm about to put you up on game."

Smooth was paying full attention.

"I just got through talking to her for almost an hour. She has decided to give it up to you tonight, and she wanted me to give her some tips," Roxy said.

Smooth licked his lips.

"Wipe that stupid grin off your face, boy. I told her everything I think she needed to know. And now I'm going to tell you the only thing I think you need to know."

"I'm listening."

"Be very gentle and take your time."

Smooth nodded his head.

"Now, what you want to talk to me about?" Roxy asked.

"I got China everything she wanted for her birthday."

"Really?"

"Yeah, I did."

"What exactly did she want?" Roxy inquired.

"A lot of shit, but the biggest and most significant is our own place."

Roxy spit out the drink she had just sipped.

"Repeat that!"

"You heard me right."

"And you think Ga Ga is going to let her move out with you?"

"That's why I need your help, sis."

"Sis, my ass! I am not getting involved with that shit. No!" Roxy shook her head.

"China's going to move out regardless of what Ga Ga says. I'm just helping her do so."

"Leave me out of that!" Roxy had spoken her mind and with that, she headed inside with Smooth behind her.

"SMOOTH," China screamed when he walked in.

Squeezing her tightly he whispered 'happy birthday' to her before he released her from his grip.

"Where's my present? Where's my present?" China chanted like an excited 5-year-old.

"Later," he replied, as he kissed her forehead.

China smiled.

Just then, the deejay played Usher's *There Goes My Baby.* Smooth pulled China in his arms and held her firmly while the singer sang his hit.

"Let's go!" Smooth led China outside.

"Close your eyes," he ordered.

Once China's eyes were closed, Smooth guided her to her first present.

"Ready?" he asked.

She nodded.

"SURPRISE!"

"Oh my God!" China screamed, jumping up and down at the sight of the black on black Range Rover.

After she calmed down a little, he handed her the keys. With trembling hands, she accepted them.

"Happy birthday, boo!"

"Thank you, thank you, thank you, baby! Thank you! Get in."

The two young lovers hopped in the truck for a quick spin.

After making it back to China's house, Smooth asked, "Are you ready for your next present?"

"There's more?"

"Yep." He reached over onto the floor of the truck behind China's seat and lifted the puppy from its box.

She excitedly grabbed the dog away from Smooth.

"He's so cute," China cooed. "Look at him. He even got on his lil' bling. You go, boy!" She held the puppy up to her face.

Smooth was pleased to see his girl so happy. He leaned over and took the locket from around the dog's neck.

"This is my favorite present from you."

He turned on the interior light, allowing China to get a good look at what he was holding in his hand.

Smooth held up the locket for China. After seeing the pictures, she began fanning her face with her free hand, trying to stop the tears.

"I had it engraved." Smooth turned is so that China could read the inscription.

China read, "Thank you for a life filled with love."

Unable to stop the tears now, China let them fall freely.

"I love you, Smooth."

"I love you more, China."

"Come on, let's get back to the party," she said.

"Hey everyone," Roxy said into the microphone. "Tonight is a very special night for a very special girl."

The crowd erupted in cheers.

Roxy waited for them to quiet down before she continued.

"Y'all cheering because y'all ain't never lived with her."

Everyone including China began laughing.

"But for real though, I do believe that I have the best little sis in the world. I love you, sugar bear." Roxy blew a kiss at her lil' sister, who returned it with one of her own.

Roxy's speech crated a domino effect. One after the other, the partygoers grabbed the microphone to say a few words to China until Ga Ga gave her speech.

"Y'all listen here," she started. "Now I don't know if my daughter thanked y'all for coming out and celebrating her special day with her. If she didn't, I want to say thank you all."

Ga Ga held up her hand.

"Don't y'all go clapping because it's already 11:00 p.m., and I want everyone out of here by 11:30. So let's cut the cake and give the birthday girl what we got for her."

Ga Ga walked inside, taking the mic with her.

"I see where you get it from," Smooth said, leaning into China's ear.

"I love my new puppy, baby, but Ga Ga's going to trip!"

"Why?" Smooth asked, feigning ignorance.

"Because it's a pit bull."

"We just won't tell her what kind of dog it is."

"Baby, she probably knows more about these dogs than we do."

"Okay, we'll just keep it ..."

"Did y'all tell Ga Ga yet?" Roxy asked, coming up on them from behind.

"Tell Ga Ga what?" China asked.

"That I got us our own place," Smooth answered nonchalantly.

"You did not!"

Smooth's only response was the keys he dangled in China's face.

"Is there any end to you?" China asked, grinning from ear to ear.

"That's it!" He threw his hands up in surrender.

"You the best, baby!"

Ga Ga came out with the birthday cake and together everyone began singing the birthday song.

"Here," Ga Ga said, as she gave the knife to China to cut the cake. Before cutting the cake, China looked around at all of the faces present because of her. She thanked God for allowing her to experience the love she felt. She looked at the starry sky, mouthed a "thank you" towards the heavens, and then allowed the knife to slice through the cake.

Everyone wondered whom the first slice would go to.

China looked at Smooth apologetically. He gave a slight nod of approval then and watched as she handed the first slice to Ga Ga.

The crowd cheered once more.

Ga Ga accepted the cake and gave her daughter a motherly hug.

"Here Roxy," China handed the knife to her sister. "Mom, can we talk?"

China led her mother inside and sat next to her on the couch.

Smooth stood next to China holding her hand.

"What is it?" Ga Ga asked.

"This is really hard for me to say," China fought to get her words out.

"Are you pregnant?"

"No, Ga Ga. I've never even had sex."

"So what is it?"

"Look, there's no easy way to say this, so I'm just going to come out with it."

"Please do!"

"I'm moving out, Ga Ga."

"Over my dead body!"

"Ga Ga, please don't make this more difficult than it already is."

"You're right," Ga Ga answered, as she got up and stalked off to her room, slamming the door behind her.

* * *

Smooth carried most of China's things out to the truck. Her mood had become sullen since her mother barricaded herself in the room. He was sure that she'd cheer up once she saw the new place.

China walked to her mother's door and tried one last time to get her to come out.

"I don't want to leave like this, Ga Ga. Can you please come out?"

Her mother's sobs were her only response.

"Come on, China," Roxy turned her around. "She'll get over it. She took it better than I expected her to. Don't let this ruin your day. Smooth's waiting to tap that."

"Shhhh, girl. What if Ga Ga hears you?"

"Girl, please. You're going to live with him," Roxy said, as she turned and walked away.

"I'll see you tomorrow," China said to the closed door.

The ride to their new place was made in mostly silence. Smooth's mind was on China and what they were about to do and China's mind was on her mother.

More than once, he'd had to tell her that the red light had changed to green.

After arriving at their new place and finally hauling the last of her things in, China allowed Smooth to give her a full tour.

"I love it!" she said.

"I was hoping you would."

"You know what I love more than this?" China said, as she kissed his lips.

"What's that?"

"My new truck."

Smooth smiled.

"But you know what I love more than my new truck?" she continued, as she kissed him again.

"What?"

"My new puppy."

"I hope you like cleaning up after him, too," Smooth teased.

"Shut up. But for real, do you know what I love more than my new home or truck or dog?"

Smooth touched the locket hanging on his girl's neck and she nodded.

"I love it more than everything else, because it shows how far we've come from and it lets me now that we'll always be together. But what I love more than anything is that YOU gave it to me. Thank you, baby."

China wrapped her arms around Smooth's neck, pulling his face to hers. He scooped her in his arms. As she wrapped her legs around his waist, he began walking towards the bedroom.

Gently, he laid her down and began undressing her. With trembling hands, he unbuttoned her skin-tight jeans and slowly pulled them down. As he made his way back up, he placed kisses on the inside of China's thighs, stopping briefly to rub his face over the mound that was inside China's G-string. Continuing on his way up, Smooth kissed his girlfriend's flat stomach and then unclasped her bra, watching as her beautiful breasts spilled free. Eagerly he took the nipple of the right breast in his mouth and sucked on it.

He squeezed her left nipple with his free hand, causing her to moan loudly. Making his way back down to her thighs, Smooth pulled the G-string off and then went to work pleasing China with his mouth. Having given her oral sex before, he knew exactly what she liked. Smooth licked his tongue into her extremely wet pussy.

"Yes, baby," China encouraged.

Smooth parted her lips with his fingers and found her clit. Knowing that she liked her clit sucked instead of licked, he began sucking right away while pumping his finger in and out of her. Slowly China began raising and lowering her pelvis to match Smooth's finger stokes.

"Just like that, baby," she cried. "I'm about to cum."

Smooth sucked harder and pumped faster. Before he knew it, China's midsection was shaking uncontrollably, and she was saying his name over and over. Smooth kept his face between her legs until she regained control of herself.

"Damn!" she said panting.

Smooth slid up, making his way to look in China's eyes. Without saying a word, he asked China if she was ready to go all the way.

She nodded.

Smooth placed the head of his penis at China's vaginal entrance and gently pushed forward.

"AAAGGGGHHH," China cried out, as her thighs instinctively tightened on Smooth.

"I'm sorry, boo," he apologized. "We don't have to do this."

"No, it's okay. Roxy said that the pain comes before the pleasure, and that we got to get past the pain if we're going to enjoy it."

China relaxed and allowed him to try again.

She closed her eyes tightly as Smooth tried again, this time getting his head in.

"Don't move."

China acted as if what she was feeling wasn't hurting too much, but she'd never felt anything like it before.

"Okay," she told Smooth, after relaxing her muscles.

Slowly he pushed forward again. This time it didn't hurt as much.

Smooth eased his way in until all eight inches of him were inside of her.

"You okay?" he asked.

China smiled, "Give me the pleasure now."

Smooth began stroking with slow rhythmic strokes and then picked up his pace after entering China for the first time; Smooth was pulling his dick out and spraying his semen onto her stomach.

"That's it?" China asked.

"Until we get cleaned up, it is. You bleeding like you just lost your virginity, girl."

"Very funny," China answered, as she slapped his chest. "Let's go take a bath."

SEVEN

Smooth sat in the passenger seat of China's truck looking out the window. He looked at his watch again and then mumbled.

"What's that?" China asked.

"Nothing. I'm just wondering where the fuck this nigga is."

"Baby, you need to relax. We'll give him 20 more minutes. If he's not here by then, we'll leave. Now chill, you're making me nervous."

"You shouldn't be here anyway. What if this is a setup or something?"

"If it is, we go out with a bang," China smiled.

Smooth didn't.

Brazen had told Smooth about Jefe or, as he liked to be called, El Jefe, an old Mexican who'd just been released from prison after serving a 10-year sentence for trafficking. He'd been Brazen's oldest brother's plug before he got sent to prison. Now that he was back on the scene, Brazen was trying to help him out in any way he could. He knew that Jefe would find his way back to the top, and when he did, Brazen was hoping that he'd remember him.

"There they are, Mr. Anxious!" China exclaimed, as she tapped Smooth's leg and pointed at the car approaching them.

Smooth and China exited the vehicle and then walked to the front to greet Brazen.

"What's good, yo?" Brazen extended his arm to Smooth, who clapped him up.

"China, what you doing here?" he asked.

"Don't question me boy, your name is not Smooth."

"Whatever, yo," Brazen said, as he turned his attention to Jefe.

"Smooth, this is El Jefe. Jefe, this is my man, Smooth I was telling you about."

The two men shook hands. Brazen ignored China.

"And who is this lovely young lady, if I may ask?" Jefe asked, turning on his charm.

"This is China," Smooth said, not willing to volunteer anything else.

"Pleased to meet you, young lady," Jefe said.

"Likewise."

"Shall we get down to business?"

"Yeah, let's do that," Smooth agreed.

"Before we do, Jefe, tell me a little about yourself," China said.

This was a first for Jefe and he was clearly caught off guard.

Brazen glared at China.

Even though he was surprised by China's request, he rebounded quickly and told her that he liked that she took the initiative to ask such a thing of him.

For 10 minutes, Jefe talked about himself. He told China about his three daughters, one of whom reminded him of her. He talked about his wife and his only son. After talking about his family, Jefe went on to talk about the fortune he'd made from selling drugs, all of which was confiscated by the government at the time of his arrest. Finally, he talked about his time in prison and the embarrassment he had to live with for the last 10 years of his life, only to be released and ostracized from the people he'd called friends, some of the very people he'd placed in their positions of power.

China listened intently. What Jefe had just shared was new information to Smooth and Brazen. However, he was simply confirming what China already knew.

Once Smooth had told her about a guy Brazen wanted him to meet who went by the name Jefe, China had hired a private investigator to do some digging. What was just said by Jefe was only part of what was uncovered. But what he didn't say spoke volumes of the man's character.

He never mentioned that he never took anyone down with him. To Jefe, keeping your mouth shut wasn't a badge of honor or something to be bragged about. It was something you did naturally like breathing.

China liked Jefe.

"Okay, let's talk business," she said, after he'd gotten through speaking.

41

"Initially I wanted to purchase 300 pounds, but I think I should purchase more," Jefe said.

"You're assuming we have more than 300 for sale," China asked.

"Yes, of course."

"That's one of the fastest ways to fail in any business venture. I will assume you're paying us $900 a pound."

"Point taken," Jefe smiled.

"What are your plans?" she asked.

"To acquire as much of your product as I can."

"And after that?"

"That does not concern you, my friend."

"You're right."

China was used to her presence dulling a man's senses, therefore giving her an advantage over them. She seemed to have no effect over Jefe, so she tried another approach.

"Let me be frank, Jefe. I know that Harlem is your stomping grounds. I also know that in the last month a pound of weed has gone from an average of $750 to more than $1,400. Now it's so bad, a person would be lucky to find more than five pounds for sale at a time."

Jefe nodded his head but remained quiet.

"So," China continued, "here's what I think you're going to do. You're going to purchase a minimum of 300 pounds from us. Since you've never been one to deal with weed, I think you're going to trade maybe 10 pounds for a kilo. The keys are only bringing in $1,700 right now in New York. Am I right?"

This was more a statement than a question.

"There is no doubt in my mind that you already have this deal lined up. So if we do the math, you'll be buying a kilo for $3,000. Three hundred pounds will get you at least 30 kilos. So for 30 kilos, all you pay is $90,000."

Jefe was impressed.

"But here's the kicker! You don't care about the weed game. Your concern is the coke; and because you're only paying $3,000, you can sell a key for thousands less than your competition and still make a

42

huge profit. He'll be competing with his own product and won't have a clue."

"Am I right?" China asked.

Jefe was amazed.

"Really, young lady, who are you?" he asked.

"So, I am right?"

"Where does that put us?" Jefe wanted to know.

"It doesn't change the prices, if that's what you're worried about."

"That doesn't answer my question."

"Okay, I'd like for you to make the same deal for us. Do you think you can make that happen?" she asked.

"And what's in it for me?"

"If you make the deal, I'll give you 100 pounds."

Jefe stuck out his hand to China. She gladly pumped it.

* * *

Several weeks had passed since China moved out of her mom's house. Since then, Ga Ga had accepted it and moved on. She'd even visited her daughter's new home on several occasions and added what she called a motherly feel to it.

Before seeing where Smooth and her daughter lived, Ga Ga worried about the type of place they could afford. After seeing it, she was even more worried. She'd worked for more than 25 years and was never able to afford anything close to what her daughter now lived in at age 16. Ga Ga wanted to know where the money was coming from to afford such a luxurious lifestyle. She'd promised herself on more than one visit that she'd ask them before she left. Today would be different though. She sat on the couch clutching her purse to her stomach waiting for Smooth or China to come home. An hour later, they came through the door laughing.

"Oh, hey Ga Ga," China said, surprised to find her mother there.

"Hey Ga Ga," Smooth said.

"I need to have a talk with y'all," Ga Ga skipped the formalities.

Smooth and China exchanged glances.

"I'm worried about y'all," she said.

"We're fine, Ga Ga," China tried to put her mother's mind at ease.

"I see that. That's what's got me so worried. You all seem to be too fine. Now I need to know what's going on around here. "

Smooth looked at China, waiting for her to answer.

"Why do you feel something is going on?" she asked her mother.

China knew exactly why her mother felt something was going on, but she needed to stall her while she thought of something plausible to tell her.

"Don't play with me, child," Ga Ga answered sternly.

Seeing that she wasn't about to get an answer from China, she turned to Smooth.

"Ga Ga, please don't make ..."

"Young man, don't you lie to me! I can't sleep at night for worrying about y'all. Now tell me what's going on," Ga Ga began weeping.

Smooth was about to tell her how he was supporting their lifestyle until China spoke up.

She knew that her mother cared for her and was concerned about her well-being, but what she was doing now was being nosy, and China had had enough.

"Mama, listen to me carefully. You have no reason at all to be losing sleep over us. I know that's you'll always have my back, and I'll be sure to tell you if and when you should start worrying. Until then, you can relax."

Ga Ga knew her daughter well enough to know that she wouldn't get anything out of her. She decided to let the matter rest. She made a mental note to catch Smooth away from China.

"Okay, young lady. If you say so," Ga Ga said, as she got up to leave.

Both China and Smooth relaxed.

"What was that?" Smooth asked once she'd left.

"You ain't seen nothing yet. She's a trip. You were about to tell her everything, too, weren't you?"

"Hell, nah."

"Yes you were."

"All I was going to tell her was that I'm serving a lil' weed."

"WHAT? Don't you do that! Don't even think about it, not with her or anyone else. Don't ever tell anyone shit! I don't believe you!"

"It's Ga Ga we're talking about, boo."

"I don't care who the hell it is. If they're not a part of it, they don't need to know anything about it!"

Just then, China's phone rang.

"Hey girl, what's up?" She shook her head at Smooth and walked away.

* * *

"It feels good to be back in the rotten apple, yo," Brazen said, as he sat back in the passenger seat of the car they'd rented for the dive to New York City. With his seat reclined as far back as it would go, he continually looked behind the car using the two side-view mirrors. With his fitted cap pulled low, it was hard to see his eyes darting from side to side.

China had assured Smooth that El Jefe would live up to his end of the bargain; therefore, it was a waste of time to escort the 700 pounds of marijuana to New York.

He wouldn't hear of it. His product would not leave his sight. So far, it hadn't. Parked next to him in the parking lot of the Burger King, where they were waiting for Jefe, was a minivan that contained the marijuana.

Jefe entered the parking lot and parked next to the van. Before getting out, he said a short prayer, something he always did before seeing a deal through. Jefe hated having to meet with Smooth in the parking lot, after having once been in the position he was in, but he was nonetheless happy for the opportunity. This was the first deal of many more that would soon follow for Jefe.

"Mi Amigos," Jefe said, as he entered the car, taking a seat behind Smooth.

The two men returned his greeting.

"Here you go," Jefe said, passing the bag to Smooth.

After taking a quick look in the bag, he gave Jefe the keys to the van.

"Jefe exited Smooth's car and walked back to his own, where he waited for the other person he was scheduled to meet.

After waiting for more than half an hour, Jefe spotted Roberto, Emilio's second-in-command, making his way out of the fast food joint and headed straight at him.

"Who are they?" Roberto asked.

"No worthless questions please, eh?"

"Were you able to deliver as promised?"

Smiling, Jefe handed him the keys to the van.

"Drive," Roberto ordered, slapping the dashboard.

Seeing Jefe's car on the move, Smooth put his car in gear and prepared to follow him until Brazen instructed him not to.

"He ain't going nowhere."

Smooth put the car in park and watched as Jefe entered the drive-thru line. Several minutes later, he was driving by again. This time, he signaled for Smooth to follow him.

Jefe drove down Flatbush Avenue until he reached his garage, the only piece of property he still owned. With the click of a button, the door opened. After both cars entered, Jefe hit the button again.

"Here we are, my friends," Jefe said, as he grabbed the bags from his back seat.

Smooth had never witnessed this much cocaine in his life, and just knowing that nearly half of it belonged to him had him smiling from ear to ear. Jefe had given away more cocaine than what was in front of him, so what he was looking at was no big deal. He was already thinking about his next move.

Brazen on the other hand was another story. He'd seen far more cocaine than what was in front of him, but he'd never been able to call this much his own. The $90,000 Jefe had given Smooth earlier along with the cocaine had Brazen's mind moving a million miles an hour. With everything in front of him, he'd be able to make all of his dreams come true, he thought. Unable to control himself, he lifted his shirt and pulled out the handgun that was concealed in his waistline.

"Y'all know what it is?" he pointed the gun at Smooth and Jefe.

Smooth shook his head. How could he have been so dumb? How did he not see this coming? He was dealing with two people he barely knew on turf that was familiar to them, not him.

"My girl trusted you, Jefe," Smooth spat out the name, as if it were poison on his tongue.

"You are mistaken badly, my friend."

"And, nigga, I trusted you."

"I'm glad you did. Now strip. You too, Chico," Brazen ordered.

Smooth began doing as he was told. First, he removed his shirt. After doing so, he noticed that Jefe hadn't made any move to disrobe. Instead, he only glared at the man in front of him holding the gun.

"Oh, you think it's a game, muthafucka?"

Brazen grabbed Jefe by the collar and drew back to strike him with the gun.

The few seconds it had taken Brazen to walk over and grab Jefe was all the time Smooth had needed to pull his gun from the small of his back. Brazen never felt the bullet that ripped through his head.

Jefe picked up the gun that fell from Brazen's hand. Smooth watched as he stood over the already dead man and shot him several more times.

"We got to get out of here," Smooth said.

"Here," Jefe said, as he handed him his share of the cocaine. "Don't worry about this cockroach. I'll take care of him."

After placing the cocaine in his car, Smooth shook Jefe's hand and made a hasty exit. He could hardly wait to get back to Florida.

* * *

"What are you doing here?" Smooth asked, surprised to see China sitting on the living room floor.

"Well, hello to you, too."

"I'm just tired. I just did 18 hours of driving."

"Brazen didn't help you drive?"

Smooth shook his head as if to say "not right now," and then he turned to Monica.

"Why you all in my mouth, girl?"

"Boy, please," Monica said.

Smooth placed his phone and keys on the table and then took a seat near China.

"I thought you were going to be at Ga Ga's crib?"

"I was, but Monica called. She was having some problems."

"Tell me something I don't know. I'm going to take a shower and get me some rest."

Just as China heard the water running, Smooth's phone began ringing.

"Hello," she answered.

"Smooth please."

"Who's calling?"

"El Jefe."

"Oh, hey Jefe, this is China. He's in the shower right now. Would you like me to give him a message or have him call you when he gets out?"

"I just wanted to make sure he arrived safely and give him my thanks."

"No thanks is needed, Jefe."

"Any time a man does what he did, many thanks are needed."

"And what, may I ask, did he do?"

"I am afraid I have already spoken too much, Señorita China. Please have him call me at his earliest convenience."

With that, the line went dead.

China put down the phone and then headed to the room that Smooth had just stepped out into from the private bathroom.

"Jefe just called," China informed him.

"What did he want?"

"To see if you made it back safely."

Smooth shook his head, smiled, and then climbed on to the bed.

"He also said that he wanted to thank you. What is he thanking you for?"

Smooth walked across the room where he closed the door. After securing the door, he relayed to her the events leading up to Brazen's death. While Smooth and China talked about his trip to New York, Monica sat in the living room bored out of her mind. To entertain herself, she picked up Smooth's phone and began playing with it.

EIGHT

Smooth sat in the driver's seat of China's truck waiting for her to exit the shoe store. Buying shoes had become a habit for China—an expensive one. He was glad that she was able to shop whenever she wanted to. Only months earlier, they had to carefully monitor their spending. Smooth smiled as she entered the truck.

"What?" China asked, returning the smile.

"I was just thinking back to when life wasn't so good for us."

"And when was that?"

"Shit, before we got this money," he answered.

"No, no, no, boo. Life has always been good for me. I've always had Roxy and you and Ga Ga. Money hasn't made my life better because I'm sure that if I was miserable before it, I'd still be miserable with it. I may be a little happier now that we got it, but it's not the root of my happiness," she said.

"Only you would look at things that way. That's why I love you so much. I got a beautiful, smart, loving woman. What more can I ask for?"

"Not much," China smiled.

"Where to, Miss Daisy?"

"Miss Daisy, my ass, boy. You mean Miss Oprah!"

"We haven't talked about our plans in a long time," Smooth said, turning serious.

"No need to."

"Come again?"

"Look, we always talked about our plans in hopes of getting a lot of money. Now that we got the money, what's the point in talking about old plans?"

"Well, maybe we need to discuss new plans to keep the money."

"Okay, what do you have in mind?" China asked.

"Nothing yet. That's why I wanted to talk to you. What would you like to do with all the money we got?"

"Nothing."

"Explain, please."

"I'm sure there's something I'd like to do with some of the money, but not all of it," China smiled, as she said this.

"Can you be serious? We need to figure out a way to keep the money coming in."

"Can we please talk about this some other time? I hate when you get all serious on me."

"I don't want to be one of those people who had it and lost it all because he didn't know what to do with it. We need to make some plans. That's all I'm saying!"

"Okay."

"Okay, what?"

"Okay, we will!" China stated emphatically.

"When?" Smooth showed no signs of letting up.

"You better be glad I love you," China said through clenched teeth.

"Sure am," he continued driving.

"Where are we going?" China asked, seeing that they weren't heading home.

"To your mom's house."

"I don't feel like it, baby," she whined.

"Make sure you tell her that once we get there. I told her we'd come by when you were in the store. By the way, when was the last time you picked up something nice for her?"

"The same time you picked up something for your mother."

In all the time Smooth had been hustling, he never once bought his mother anything. As far as he was concerned, she didn't deserve anything—not even the air she breathed. Smooth was only seven years old when his mom had first gone to prison for three counts of child abuse. The abuse had started long before he was seven, but had gotten so bad that it could not be ignored any longer. Smooth's teacher had reported the abuse after he entered the classroom with a black eye and a small gash on his head. After being examined, it was revealed that Smooth had numerous cigarette burn marks on his body. It was even clear that someone had placed a hot iron right in the middle of the boy's back. When asked who had done it, he never said a word. He was much more afraid of his mother than he was of the adults who were questioning him.

Smooth and his two younger siblings were removed from his mother's care and given to his aunt, who was just as abusive to them as their mother was. However, their aunt's abuse was verbal.

After serving her sentence, his mother petitioned the court to regain custody of her three kids who she loved more than her own self. After completing all of the court's stipulations, she received custody. Two weeks later, she hit Smooth in the back with a bullwhip because he'd come in the house two minutes later than when she told him to. At 12 years old now, he had enough and decided to fight back. That was a mistake on his part. His mother beat him within inches of his life. The last time he had spoken to her was at her sentencing. Smooth read from a letter he'd written to her. When he'd finished, there wasn't a single dry eye in the courtroom. As the bailiff led her away, he screamed out, "I hate you!" The courtroom erupted in applause. Smooth had never seen his mother since and only rarely did he think about her.

"If my mother cared for me only half as much as Ga Ga cares for you, I'd make sure she always had money on her books. Then again, if she cared, she wouldn't be in there for beating me damn near to death."

"I didn't meant anything by it, baby."

"I'm sure you didn't."

For the rest of the ride, they both remained silent.

* * *

More than a month had passed since Smooth first attempted to talk with China about their future plans, yet they still had not had the conversation.

China was content with the way things were going, and she didn't want to jinx it by talking about anything else.

They'd finally run out of the weed they had gotten from Boss' warehouse, which suited China just fine. The cocaine they were now moving was more to her liking. No matter how hard she tried, she couldn't figure out how Jefe had come up so quickly. He had made it back to the top just as quickly as he had fallen. He wasn't exactly on top, but he was almost there. To show his appreciation to Smooth and China, he made a deal with them that would guarantee they pay no more than $10,000 a kilo. The only stipulation was that they had to purchase no less than 30 kilos a month. If they ever failed to do so, the deal would be broken.

China had even taken a more active role in getting rid of the product. She wanted to be present for every deal Smooth made and she'd even made deals on her own. On more than one occasion, Smooth had tried to put his foot down, only to have it picked up by China. He hated to admit it, but she was far better than he was at their trade.

They both sat on the couch watching *Belly* for the millionth time when the doorbell rang.

"I'll get it," China jumped to her feet.

Without waiting for an answer, she opened the door. Standing on the other side was Monica, with what looked like enough suitcases to fill a small boutique.

It was obvious that she'd been crying a lot.

China pulled her friend into her arms.

"Get her stuff," she ordered Smooth.

Obediently, he got up from the couch.

"Talk to me," China told her friend, as she pulled out a chair for her at the kitchen table.

"There goes my night," Smooth mumbled to himself.

He turned off the movie and then headed to the bedroom where he grabbed his books.

"Can y'all take that to the room?" he asked as he came into the kitchen.

After they walked off, Smooth sat down at the table and spread out his books. As he did so, he noticed what he thought were Monica's tears, and for the first time wondered what was wrong with her.

Monica's mom had been into a horrible car accident and was now in the hospital hooked up to life support. The doctor said that she was completely braindead.

Monica had fallen to the ground after hearing the news, only to be picked up by Duwan, her mother's boyfriend of almost 10 years.

It was Duwan who provided food and shelter for her and her siblings when her mother couldn't find a job. Even though she was the only one that wasn't Duwan's biological child, he never made her feel like she wasn't. She had grown to love him, as she would've loved her real father.

As he held her tightly, he promised that they'd get through the ordeal together as a family.

"You have to pick up where your mom left off, Monica."

"I will," she answered in between sobs.

"You will."

"Yes, sir."

Duwan's next words were lost to Monica. She couldn't think of anything besides the bulge that was pressing against her body. Feeling uncomfortable, she tried to break free from his embrace, only to be held tighter.

"Stop Duwan, please!"

"I've watched you grow from a little girl to a young lady to a grown woman, and I've wanted you for so long. I even fantasized about you while I did it with your mother, just wondering what it would be like if it were you that my cock was sliding in and out of. Can you feel it?" he asked, as he pressed up against her even harder.

"Please don't do this."

"Tonight my fantasies will come true. No more sneaking looks at you or smelling your underwear."

He placed his face in the crook of Monica's neck and then licked on her. She squirmed trying to break free.

As she tried to break free, there was a knock at the door. He signaled for Monica to be quiet.

"Who is it?" she screamed out.

"It's Donna."

Donica—or Donna, which is what everyone called her—was

Monica's mother's friend.

"You better not say a word of this to her." Duwan put on his best sad face and opened the door.

Monica used the time that Duwan and Donna talked to pack up all of her belongings and call a taxi.

When the taxi arrived, she'd given the driver China's address and cried whole way there.

    * * *

After listening and consoling her friend as best she could, China looked at her watch.

"I got to go take care of something. If you need anything, let Smooth know. I'll be back in about an hour," China said on her way out.

"Where you going?" Smooth asked, noticing that China had picked up her keys and cell phone.

"To the store. I got to get a few feminine products for Monica."

"Grab me ice cream."

Knowing that he'd decline, China asked, "You want to come with me?"

Smooth only shook his head.

"See you when I get back." She kissed him and walked out.

On the way to Duwan's house, China checked and re-checked the magazine in her small Beretta several times. She always knew the day would come when Duwan would finally hit on Monica. Had it not been for Donna arriving when she did, he would've violated her friend in the worst way. She turned on the interior light, applied some lip-gloss, and then stepped out.

"Hi D, is Monica here?" China asked, as she stepped past him and entered the house, not waiting for an answer.

"No. She ... um ... she ... um ... just went to the store I think. She said she'd be right back. Why don't you have a seat and wait on her."

China was already sitting.

"Duwan took a seat opposite her.

"Where's Marvin and Marlin?" China asked, referring to Monica's little twin brothers.

"They're at my mother's house.

"So you're all alone?" China inquired, biting her bottom lip.

"Just me and you," Duwan said, stepping closer to China.

"That's what I wanted to hear."

"Yeah? Why is that?" Duwan rubbed his crotch.

"Come to the room. Let me show you."

He walked behind China slapping her lightly on the ass. China had always disliked being around Duwan. The way he licked his lips whenever Monica walked by him indicated to China that sooner or later the day would come when he'd make his move.

In the room, China turned around to see Duwan unbuttoning his pants.

"What are you doing?" she pointed at his hands.

"I'm undressing for you ... for us. For that good stuff you got here, girl."

"I'm going to do all of that for you. You just lay on the bed," China ordered.

Duwan rushed over to the bed to do as he was told.

"Lay on your stomach. I want to give you a massage."

Duwan rolled over.

China climbed onto the bed and straddled his back. Feeling the weight of China on his back made him smile. She removed the gun from her clutch bag.

"You ready for this?" China asked.

He nodded his head.

China placed the pillow over his head; and before he had the opportunity to say anything about it, she fired a round into his head.

She climbed off the bed and then picked up the pillow to inspect her work. Not satisfied, she walked into the kitchen and came back with a filet knife she had seen Monica's mom use quite often. She placed the knife at Duwan's neck and yanked upward as hard as she could. Now satisfied, she walked over to the drawer, and using her shirt, she pulled out a pair of socks.

Dropping the knife in the sock, she walked out.

On her way back home, China stopped at the store to buy a few things.

* * *

"What are you studying?" Monica asked Smooth.

"Something you don't know anything about," Smooth responded.

"I know a lot more than you know I do."

"Yeah, well I don't think you know anything about this."

"Well, if I don't, you can teach me," Monica said, as she pulled out a chair.

She looked so pitiful, so Smooth allowed her to stay seated.

"Okay, welcome to the world of investments. Would you like to talk about stocks and bonds or CDs? Maybe you'd like to talk about commodities?"

Smooth tried to make it all sound like uninteresting stuff.

"Let's start with the stocks," Monica said.

"You just don't give up, do you?"

"I actually know this stuff."

"Right."

"For real! See this chart right here? You're actually following the wrong stock."

"And what makes you say that?" Smooth asked.

"What most likely caught your attention with this stock right here is the fact that it rose so quickly after its initial public offering."

"If you don't sell quickly, you'll lose money."

"How do you know that?"

"It's all public hype. Most investors don't do their own research on companies they invest in. Look at this," Monica said, picking up one of the papers lying on the table.

"The company sells jewelry for dogs. How many dogs do you see wearing jewelry?"

She was right again.

"So the company was made to sound good to investors and it did. But just as quickly as people bought into it, they buy out. So the faster you sell, the more you'll save. Trust me."

Smooth had never taken the time to sit and talk with Monica, but he was glad that he did so now.

"Okay, Ms. Guru," he smiled. "Tell me, what should I be looking for if I want to invest some money?"

"Honestly, what you should be looking for is a good stockbroker. But if you're hell bent on trying this thing yourself, I suggest you start off slow and get the feel of it."

"Then?"

"You always want to look at types of companies first, not the company itself."

"Explain that."

"Okay, you have retailers that sell grocery. That's the type of company. Now look for which retail grocery store is outselling its competition. If it's appealing to you, you look into why it's doing better than the others are. That's the reason why you should invest or not invest."

"Wow. You just impressed the shit out of me. I didn't know you had it in you."

"You never gave me a chance to impress you. And like I said, I know a lot more than you think I do," Monica replied, looking at Smooth with puffy eyes.

"Why haven't you invested some money and made a killing?"

"And just where do you think I'm going to get the money from?" she asked.

"Good question."

"I see the way you and my girl got it going on up in here, and I tell myself that I'll have this and so much more. I just got to get my start."

Smooth was about to say something until China came through the door.

"Took you long enough!" he said, taking the bag from her hand.

"We'll finish this little chat some other time."

Smooth walked to the room eating his ice cream.

Shortly after Smooth entered the room, China came in behind him. "I'm glad y'all getting along."

"Why wouldn't we be?" he asked.

"Why haven't y'all been getting along," China returned with a question of her own.

"I can see that she got some shit going on, so I decided to take it easy on her."

"That was nice of you," China said, as she began removing her clothes to take a shower.

"You want to tell me what's going on now?"

"Monica's mom was in a terrible accident and now ..."

"I'm not talking about that. I'm talking about where you just came from?"

"You know where I just came from. I came from the store."

"That's it?"

China thought for a second before answering.

"Yeah, that's it!"

"Okay, but just remember, you started it!" Smooth was visibly hurt.

"Started what?"

"You leave out of here saying you're going to the store that's five minutes away. You come back an hour and half later with a few items in a bag, but I'm supposed to believe that you only went to the store?"

"Why the fuck wouldn't you believe me if that's what I told you?"

"Who the fuck do you think you're talking to?" Smooth shouted, and got up from the edge of the bed.

"I'm talking to you mutha ..."

Smooth's hand connected with the side of China's face.

"Where were you?"

"Why do you think I went anywhere else?" she cried.

Smooth grabbed her by her upper arms and pulled her to her feet.

"This is why!"

He raised her right hand to her eyes. China stared in disbelief at the dried blood on her hand.

NINE

China had never lied to Smooth and she wished she hadn't that night. Since then, things had taken a turn for the worse in their relationships. Three days had passed since he slapped her and she lied to him. Three days and there was very little that he said to her. Whenever he did talk to her, it was only in response to something she'd asked him. China hated the treatment she had been receiving from him, but she accepted it because she knew she deserved it. Still, she wanted to know when it would end, so she tried everything from sex to cooking.

Smooth declined it all.

"How long are you going to treat me like this?" she asked.

Smooth was also tired of the awkward silence between him and his girl. He also wanted to end it, but he couldn't allow it to just yet. China needed to be taught a lesson.

"Until I get tired. Or you get tired."

"Whatever," she replied, then got up and stormed off.

"What are you up to?" he approached Monica, as she tapped away on the computer.

"Nothing much. Just talking to my girl in Japan."

"What's she telling you? How to cook sweet and sour cat?"

"Ha-ha. You ain't funny. She's telling me about what's hot and what's not in technology. You know we follow them with that shit."

"That's pretty smart. But what do you care about that? The only technology you got is your phone!"

Monica shook her head. I care because if I know what's hot, I'll know what company is making the hot shit."

A light bulb went off in Smooth's head.

"Here's what I'm going to do for you. I'm going to give you $10,000 to try your hand with the real thing. Let's see if you can back up all that shit you been talking."

Monica looked behind her to make sure China was nowhere within earshot before she spoke, "All I need is a chance and I'll show you I can back it up."

Her message was clear to Smooth.

In the time that China and Smooth hadn't been speaking, he lavished attention on Monica and she enjoyed every minute on it. When he was asleep or not at home, Monica researched companies and learned as much as she possibly could about the stock market, in hopes that she'd be able to continue impressing him.

Smooth had a tingle in his balls as Monica spoke and decided that he needed to get over his issues with China before he did something he didn't want to.

"You still at it, huh?" he asked.

He turned around and walked into the room he and China shared. He picked up the remote and turned off the TV.

"I was watching that," China spoke with an attitude.

"You said it right, you *was*."

China rolled her eyes.

"Why did you lie to me?"

"Don't ..."

"Answer my question, China."

"I needed to take care of something."

"Which was?"

"Smooth, it had nothing to do with our relationship or our business. And if you think I cheated on you, you're wrong."

"What did you do, China?"

She remained tight-lipped.

"Oh, I guess since I wasn't a part of it, I don't need to know about it, huh?"

"Exactly, baby."

The hurt in his eyes was evident.

Smooth knew that China was secretive by nature, but he never thought that she'd purposely hold things back from him, especially if he asked her. Now that she had, it was time for him to do some re-evaluating. The way things were going, he was sure they'd get worse before they got better.

Maybe he was overreacting, he thought. After all, it was China he was talking to himself about. The same China who would take her last bit of money and give it to him. The same China who never allowed anyone to say a bad word about him. His China who'd always go without to make sure he had.

It was those reasons and more that made him wonder what the hell was going on. Why was she hiding things from him? Was she hiding things from him all along and just making it seem as if she shared everything with him? What else was she hiding?

The questions kept coming.

"I'm going for a drive," he told her.

"Alright," China said, as she turned on the TV as he walked out.

* * *

"Hello, may I speak with Ms. Burkley, please, "Smooth asked.

"May I ask who's calling," the sleeping voice replied.

"It's Donavan Johnson."

Silence lined the other end.

"How does Ms. Burkley know you?"

"Look, Ms. Burkley, this is the young dude you told to get some credit cards instead of walking around with so much cash."

Ms. Burkley smiled, finally able to place a face to the voice on the other end.

"Oh, I'm sorry. What's up? What can I do for you?"

"I need your help finding another place."

"You're calling me at grown-folks hours to discuss something we can discuss during normal business hours?"

"I'm tripping. You're right! What time does your office open?"

"Normally at 8:00 a.m., but if you need me, I'll be there before then."

"I guess I can wait."

"Do you want to talk about it now, or do you want me to force it out of you when you come to the office?"

"It's that obvious, huh?"

"No. Where are you?"

"Cruising the streets."

"You sound like you can use a friend. Why don't you go back to your building and call me when you're on the 24th floor."

"What's on the 24th floor?" he asked.

"If you really want to know, young man, you'll go there like I told you to," Ms. Burkley hung up.

Ten minutes later, Smooth dialed Ms. Burkley's number.

"That was quick," she said, after her told her he had just stepped off the elevator.

"Hang on a second," she told him.

Smooth held the phone to his ear waiting for her to come back on the line.

"Hello."

Smooth looked to where the voice was coming from and was surprised to see Ms. Burkley standing in the hallway.

"What are you doing here?" he asked as he approached her.

"I live here."

"Since when?"

"Since my father died and left me this building."

"You own all this?"

"This and a lot more. Come inside. I don't think my neighbor would approve of me standing in the hallway at almost midnight talking to a young man in my robe."

"So take the robe off," Smooth joked.

"Get in here." She pulled him by the arm.

"Would you like something to drink?" she asked him, while pouring herself a shot of Hennessy on the rocks.

"No. Alcohol for me is a no-no."

"That's rare. But it's not bad at all. Here, just taste it."

Smooth shook his head.

"Come on, it won't do anything to you. Then at least you'll be able to say you tried it but didn't like it."

He agreed with her then reached for the glass. The liquid felt like fire being poured down his throat.

He began coughing. After his coughing spell was over, he asked for his own glass.

"Oh, my God! I've created a monster," Ms. Burkley laughed.

Smooth smiled, but there was sadness in his eyes.

"So what's on your mind?" she asked.

"Your life is so perfect. I don't think you'd understand."

"And what do you know about my life?"

"I know that you're young, rich, and beautiful," he answered.

"Young ... yes. Rich ... maybe. Beautiful ... no."

"Are you for real? Man, I know a thousand niggas that would love to be with a chick like you."

"Where are they?" she asked.

"You looking at one."

"Yeah, right. I've seen your girlfriend, and there's no way I can compete with that."

"You make it sound as if you're an ugly duckling or something."

"Let's change the subject please."

"Nah, let's stay right where we are," Smooth said.

He rose from his seat and walked over to where Ms. Burkley stood.

"I've wanted to touch your body from the very first time I laid eyes on you."

"Why didn't you?"

Smooth accepted the invitation and then planted his lips on hers. As they kissed, he untied her robe.

"Ms. Burkley, you're beautiful!" he said, as she stared at her naked body beneath the robe.

"Call me Miranda."

She allowed him to push the robe over her shoulders, causing it to fall to the ground.

Smooth leaned forward alternating between placing kisses and sucking on her neck. As he did so, he turned Miranda around. Now with her back to his stomach, he grabbed a handful of her breast and squeezed her nipple. Miranda grinded her ass against the bulge in Smooth's pants, as he made circles around her clit with his free hand.

She placed her hands behind her back and unfastened his belt buckle and then his pants. She turned around once she felt his pants fall. Lowering herself to her knees, Miranda pulled Smooth's boxers down.

Before taking him into her mouth, she stroked his nice-sized dick several times while looking into his eyes as if seeking permission.

Smooth placed his hand on her head to guide it to his throbbing dick. Miranda's mouth reminded him of the liquid fire he drank a few minutes earlier. The pleasure was too much, causing his knees to buckle.

This made her smile.

"You need to sit down."

Once Smooth had taken a seat, Miranda went back to work, burying her face in his lap. With both hands on his dick, she sucked the head while jacking it with both hands.

Continuing to hold his dick with both hands, Miranda sucked Smooth's balls into her mouth and began twirling around them with her tongue.

"Damn girl!" was all he was able to say.

Miranda decided she'd played around long enough. She placed her hands on his chest and pushed him backward. Leaving her hands where they were, she took his dick into her mouth and began deep throating him.

Smooth was amazed that she was able to take all of him in. Miranda went faster and faster until she felt his dick twitching in her mouth. She sucked on the head, as Smooth let out a powerful orgasm.

"Shit!" Smooth gritted his teeth.

Not one to be outdone, he changed positions with her and spread her legs as far apart as they'd go. Miranda's neatly shaved pussy was inviting Smooth to take a taste. Happily he did. Smooth lapped up some of the thick white cream oozing from Miranda's love tunnel and then stuck his tongue inside of her. After fucking her with his tongue, Smooth began flicking his tongue over Miranda's clit. Seeing her response prompted him to go faster.

"Keep doing that," she said while rubbing his head.

Smooth enjoyed the control he temporarily held over her.

"Put your fingers in it," she coached.

She allowed Smooth to do what he was going for a few minutes, before she gave him his next order.

"Now slide one finger in my ass."

He did as she ordered.

"Shit yeah, baby, just like that. Keep doing it."

Smooth had never done anything like that with China, but he was absolutely enjoying Miranda's teaching.

"Ohhhh, fuck, I'm cumming," she cried, as she pulled the back of Smooth's head firmly between her legs.

"Oh, Donavan," she cried.

Smooth hardly ever heard his real name, and hearing it now from her brought a smile to his face.

After the powerful orgasm, Miranda laid back panting like an animal that had just run for its life.

"Where did you learn to do that?" she asked.

He only smiled.

"I need a drink."

Seeing Miranda walk across the room wearing nothing but an anklet made Smooth touch his dick. He was eager to feel his dick inside her. He waited for her to make her way back over to him.

"I see your soldier is still standing at attention," she said.

Miranda turned around so that he'd be able to get a good look at her ass. After straddling him, she took his dick in her hand and then slowly lowered herself on it. Smooth watched as inch after inch of his dick disappeared into her tight pussy.

"You like it this way?" she questioned, moved up and down slowly.

Smooth nodded.

"Or do you like it this way?" Miranda asked, moving up and down faster, slapping her ass cheeks against his thighs.

Smooth nodded again.

Miranda placed her palms on the floor of her to brace herself, and then continued throwing her ass at him as fast as she could.

The sight of her ass and his dick going in and out of her, along with the intense pleasure he was feeling, was more than enough to make him cum again.

Smooth enjoyed the position right up to the moment he was about to cum, and then he pulled out.

"Get on the couch," he ordered.

Miranda did as she was told.

Smooth entered her again from behind, but this time he was in control. He held her by the waist as he slid in and out. Slow than faster.

"Beat this pussy!"

He continued pumping.

"That's all you got?"

Smooth rammed his dick into her as hard as he could.

"That's how I like it. Give me that dick!"

"Hearing her talk like that was a major turn on for him. The Miranda that was on her knees now begging to be fucked hard was a completely different Miranda from the one he'd met at the office. The contrast turned him on even more.

Before long, she was crying out in pleasure again. But he hadn't cum.

"Still standing, huh?" Miranda said, after seeing Smooth was still hard.

She went to her room and came back with a small tube of lubricant.

"What's that for?" Smooth eyed her suspiciously.

"My secret weapon."

Miranda lubed her asshole and then got back into the position Smooth had just fucked her in and wiggled her ass.

"I don't know about that."

"Come on and try! If you don't like it, we'll stop."

Smooth stood behind her and then watched as she guided his dick to her ass. Smooth had no idea what to expect. But he found himself enjoying the feel of Miranda's ass.

What had Smooth cumming in minutes was the way she constantly worked her muscles. After releasing his orgasm, he collapsed on top of her, not bother to pull out.

* * *

When Smooth returned home, the place was in complete darkness, just as he'd hoped. Even though he and China weren't communicating right then, he didn't believe he could face her after what he just got through doing.

After getting a drink of water, Smooth pulled off his shirt, walked over to the couch, and lay down.

Before falling asleep, images of the lady on the 24th floor entered his mind. He fell asleep smiling.

What felt like 10 minutes later, but was actually closer to five hours, Smooth was awakened by China's puppy's growls. Zorro tore Smooth's shirt into pieces.

Ignoring the shirt, he got up and headed to the room that he and China shared, only to find China not there and a note on the bed. He read the note:

I'll be at Ga Ga's if you need me. Call or come by. Roxy and I are taking her out for a special girl's day. I would've told you earlier but sis called after you left last night, and I didn't want to wake you up. I love you, baby.

Smooth balled up the note and tossed it in the trash. He was glad that she left. He lightly tapped on Monica's door.

"Yeah," she answered from across the room.

He waited for her to open the door.

Monica opened the door holding a five-pound dumbbell in each hand, and still following along with the instructor on the DVD.

"What's up?" she raised one leg and then the other.

"Oh my bad, I wasn't trying to disturb you. I just wanted to give you this." He handed her an envelope containing $10,000.

"You were for real!" Monica replied in shock.

"Yeah, I was for real. Just make sure you use that for what it's for."

"I will. By the way, what do I owe you for this?"

"Well, if you're as good as you say you are, then I should be seeing millions by tomorrow."

They both laughed.

"You don't owe me nothing. Just do you."

"I've been doing me for too long now. I'm ready to do something else."

Monica's message was loud and clear. Smooth stared at the beads of sweat as they disappeared into Monica's cleavage.

He shook his head, breaking her spell on him and then walked away.

"Smooth," Monica called, as she went after him.

"It's not going to happen."

"Let me just say something to you."

"Talk."

"I love my girl China to death. God knows I do. I can't remember one single time when I needed her and she wasn't there for me. That's my girl and I'd die for her. She knows it."

"So that's why you keep pushing up on me?" he laughed.

"That's the thing. I can't help this shit. Every time you come around, my body goes through some shit. I wish that I could help it, but I can't. China doesn't deserve me to betray her this way, and I don't want to. Had you been anybody else, this wouldn't be an issue, but I'm stuck on you. Always have been."

"Monica, you a trip!"

"Put all that side what I just told you. China doesn't deserve you. She's my girl and all, but she'll do you more harm than good in the long run."

"And I guess you deserve me?" Smooth asked.

"China's an angel compared to me, so if she doesn't deserve you, I definitely don't!"

With that, she returned back to her workout.

TEN

Smooth had finally sold the last of the weed. He was glad to have it all gone ... and so was China. Once they started copping from Jefe, China looked at the weed as a big headache.

Smooth sat on the floor with the money machine in front of him waiting to be fed another mouthful of bills.

Smooth had sent China shopping and ordered her to take Monica with her.

So far, he'd been at his task for more than seven hours. Separating the bills had taken a long time and he was glad to have that part past him.

After wrapping the large wads of cash with thick rubber bands, Smooth threw them in one of two piles.

He still had a long way to go, so he showed no signs of letting up. As he placed another wad into the machine, his phone rang. As he looked at the screen, he saw China's face. He hit the send button.

"Talk to me."

"Can we come home now?"

"No, I thought I told you I'd call you."

"What's with the attitude, nigga?"

Smooth hung up the phone, ignoring China's question, and went back to work.

Three hours later, he was finished. Smooth had counted just under $3.3 million. He picked up the phone and called China.

"What?" she answered.

"I'm finished," was all he said.

Smooth carried the two large bags back to the room. He then unplugged the money counter and carried that back to the room as well.

There was more money sitting in the closet than he'd thought. He knew that they were making money, but he also knew that they were spending a lot of it.

He laid back and waited for China to arrive.

When she finally walked in, Zorro ran to greet her, jumping up and down. After putting her bags down, she picked up her dog and played with him for a few seconds. As soon as she put him down, he ran over to his bowl and brought it to her.

China filed both of his bowls and then headed to her room.

"You could've at least fed the fucking dog."

"Damn, I forgot," Smooth said, as he got up and headed to the kitchen.

"I already did it."

Smooth turned around.

"How much?" China asked.

"Three million two hundred and ninety thousand dollars," he answered, giving her the exact number.

She smiled.

"We're doing good," she said.

"I know. Better than we expected. Better than we ever imagined at 16."

"I agree."

"That's why I think it'll be best if we quit now."

China was definitely not trying to hear that.

The thrill of being a drug dealer was addictive to China. The pull was too strong. Even if she wanted to, she couldn't stop. And she had no intention of stopping.

"Smooth, I think we should continue doing what we're doing. Things are going perfect for us. Why stop now?"

"You just answered your own question. We stop now because things are going perfect. What, you think we should wait until things go bad? If that's the case, we won't have to stop. It'll stop us."

What Smooth said made sense, but it wasn't what she wanted to hear. Smooth saw it in her face.

"I'm not trying to convince you one way or the other, boo. You can do whatever you like. I'm just telling you that I'm through. I don't want anything to do with it anymore."

Smooth walked to the closet and pulled out the two bags. He tossed one at China's feet.

"That's your half."

She wasn't sure of what to say. On one hand, she had the money to continue doing what she wished; on the other hand, she looked at the splitting of the money as a split between her and Smooth. She didn't want to be without him.

China knelt down and unzipped the bag. After taking a look inside, she got up.

"So, what does this mean for us?" she asked.

"Nothing," Smooth replied, as he opened his arms and pulled her in. She never saw the lone tear that fell from his eye and came to rest on her head.

Neither did he see the tears that disappeared into the fabric of his shirt. They both knew that the beginning of the end had arrived.

* * *

The following day, Smooth placed a call to El Jefe to notify him of the things going on with China and himself.

The call was done out of respect. Anytime China had called him, he'd wait to also receive a call from Smooth. If the call didn't come, he'd call Smooth to bring him abreast of everything.

Smooth felt obligated to do the same.

After being placed on hold for two minutes, Smooth finally heard Jefe's voice.

"Mi amigo!"

"What's up, Jefe?"

"This is not a common call, so why don't you tell me. But please my friend, be careful," Jefe referred to the phone line.

"Well, there's been a small change. My girl and I are no longer partners."

"This cannot be so. You two are perfect co-workers. What happened?"

"I've decided to call it quit. I did well for myself, but I never intended to make a career of it."

"Smart move, kid. Smart move. It's like playing craps. You keep rolling the dice and sooner or later, you crap out. I like you a lot, my friend. I hope our paths cross again in the future. If not, good luck."

"Thank you, Jefe. I guess this is goodbye then."

"Never goodbye, my friend. Never goodbye. So long for now."

"Okay then," Smooth said. "So long for now."

"This number is always good for you, my friend. So long for now."

With that, they both hung up their phones.

Smooth dialed another number, but this time the person who he wanted to talk to answered the phone.

"What's up?" he asked Miranda.

"Nothing much, just balancing the books."

"Why don't you let one of your underlings do that so I can take you to lunch?"

"You can take me to lunch, but no one balances the books but me."

"So what time should I pick you up?" he asked.

"I'll be ready whenever you get here."

"I'm on my way."

Before leaving to meet Miranda, Smooth slid open the balcony door so that Zorro could relieve himself. Next, he filled the dog's bowls and headed out the door.

* * *

"Am I too early?" he asked, walking through the door to her office.

"No, not at all," Miranda said, walking around her desk to give him a hug.

"You ready?"

"Let me go to the ladies room and I'll be right out."

While she was gone, Smooth looked around her office at the many plaques and pictures. One picture was of a younger Miranda with her arms wrapped around an older man who she resembled greatly.

"That's my daddy," she said, walking up on Smooth.

The love and respect for the man in the picture was clear in her voice.

"So where to?" she asked.

"I was hoping you know of some place we could go."

"I do," she answered without hesitation.

"Somewhere black," Smooth added.

"Boy, please! Let's go!"

Miranda volunteered to drive; instead of getting in Smooth's car, hey headed over to Miranda's.

She maneuvered out of her parking lot and then gunned it up the street, as Sade's music drifted from the speakers.

Thus far, Smooth liked everything about the lady. He reclined his seat, closed his eyes, and smiled.

"What are you smiling at?" she asked.

"I like this car," he lied.

"Is that really what you're smiling about?"

"That's not it!"

"What is it then?" she wanted to know.

"I called my connect earlier and told him that I was done."

"And what made you do that?"

"I surpassed my goal. I got enough money to go all the way legit."

"That's good for you," she slapped his thigh.

"Yeah, no more looking over my shoulder."

Miranda was highly impressed by the young man sitting in her car.

"So now what?"

Smooth had thought of several things but hadn't made any plans to pursue any of his ideas. He was fairly certain about investing in the stock market, so he shared his thoughts on that with her.

"I'm going to try my hand at the stock market. Invest maybe a hundred stacks into that and see what it does."

Miranda frowned at his idea.

"Why not try something a little more sound, where you stand to make good money."

"What's that?" Smooth asked, liking the way it sounded.

"Real estate," she suggested.

"I don't now shit about real estate, so why would ..."

"You didn't know shit about selling drugs either until you learned, right?"

"Yeah, but!"

"But nothing. You sound like the typical young black man now. You can learn whatever you want to. You just got to apply yourself."

Smooth remained quiet. The smile was gone from his face now.

"Yeah, I do," he answered honestly.

"Good, I'll teach you. But let's eat first, I'm starving."

They got out of the car and headed inside the restaurant. Because of lunch hour being at its peak, Glenda's was full to capacity. Smooth and Miranda waited outside to be seated. Several groups of people left before being called in to be seated.

"I've been waiting to talk to you about this," Miranda said, as she took her seat while moving her hand back and forth.

"What about us?" Smooth asked.

"What's going on here?"

"I'm not sure I know what you mean?"

"Smooth, we need to draw some lines. I need some clarity."

"Why? I thought things were fine."

"Well, you're wrong. The sex with you is great, but I'm not someone that gets absorbed with sex. I need more than that out of a relationship. And I definitely can't be your girl on the side."

Smooth pinched the bridge of his nose.

"So what are you telling me ... to leave China?"

"No, not at all. I'm telling you that as long as there is a you and China, there can't be a you and me. Not sexually anyway. I deserve someone to call my own."

"I wasn't expecting this," Smooth said.

The sex with Miranda was incomparable to anything he'd ever experienced, and the thought of it not happening any more wasn't something he was happy about.

"I'm not asking you to do anything. I just needed to tell you how I felt about things. Now that we won't be having sex, you won't think it's something you did."

He nodded his head in acceptance.

"One last time then?"

Miranda let out a loud burst of laughter.

"No. Let's order, silly" she slapped his hand lightly.

* * *

Smooth opened the door and was surprised to find Monica at her favorite spot tapping away at the keyboard.

"What's up?" he spoke first.

"China is pissed you," she warned

"What's new?"

"SMOOTH, IS THAT YOU?" China screamed.

Without answering, he walked to the room.

"Yeah, it's me. Who else you thought it was?"

"I've been calling your phone all day," she said, with her hands on her hips.

"What else have you been doing all day?"

"What is that supposed to mean?"

He ignored her question and began talking off his clothes.

"Smooth, what have you been doing all day?" she asked.

"You don't need to know," he responded.

"Why the hell not?"

Before answering, he looked at China with a smile.

"For one, you're not my mother, and, two, you weren't a part of it. You know how that goes. If you weren't a part of it, you don't need to know about it." He'd been waiting to use her words on her.

"So that's how you want to play, huh? Okay, don't ask me shit from here on out, muthafucka!"

Smooth smiled again, shrugged his shoulders, and then headed to the bathroom. He turned around just in time to catch China's phone as she threw it at him.

"Coolly, he tossed it on the bed.

"That's always been one of your flaws. You can't take what you give out. I got news for you, the world doesn't move to your beat."

Smooth stepped into the bathroom, locking the door behind him.

"The world don't, but you do," China said, just above a mumble.

Smooth stepped in the shower and rotated his shoulders as the water massaged him. He thought about Miranda. She was everything he hoped China would be when she got older. It was easy for him to picture himself being with her. She was very independent but also submissive. Smooth loved that about her. Things had been at their lowest with him and China and he was tired of her acting as if she owned him. He admitted that she owned his heart though. He loved China; and even though they'd been at it with each on a daily basis, he couldn't see himself without her.

Smooth wrapped the towel around his waist and stepped out of the bathroom to find China stuffing clothes into a small suitcase.

"I'm going to see Jefe," she answered the question in his eyes.

"Why are you telling me your business?" he answered.

"You can be such an asshole sometimes."

"That's me, Mr. Asshole. And your name is ..." he smiled.

China picked up the suitcase and walked out

* * *

"It's good to see you again, China," Jefe said, as she entered the room accompanied by two of Jefe's bodyguards.

"It's good to see you also," she extended her hand.

"How was your trip?"

"Not bad. Except for the accident on the turnpike, it was smooth sailing."

Jefe nodded his head. He knew all about the accident. He knew exactly where China was at all times, thanks to the tracking device he'd had logged to her car. It wasn't China alone he took precautions with; he did the same thing to everyone that he sold to.

"How many times did you have to stop for gas?" he asked.

China was used to the questions, but still she hated it.

"Three times. My car's good on gas."

"Are you hungry? Let's have a bite to eat."

"Jefe headed toward the kitchen with China in tow.

After instructing his chef on what he'd like, he turned to China and asked, "What will you be having?"

"What are my options?"

"You say it, he prepares," Jefe replied, with a snap of his fingers.

China ordered something she knew wouldn't take long to fix and wouldn't taste bad.

"I'll have a grilled cheese, light on the mayonnaise."

Jefe smiled. He knew the sandwich was ordered simply out of courtesy, not to offend him.

"How have you been since we last met?" Jefe asked.

"Real good, thank you for asking. And how have you been?" China returned the question.

"Business is good. I cannot complain. My wife refuses to have anything to do with me as long as I'm in the life and she forces this on my kids also. What can I do?" Jefe asked rhetorically.

Jefe's words made China think about Smooth. She felt a thud in her heart. She promised herself that she'd make things right with him when she got back home.

Jefe caught the far-away look on China's face and decided not to interrupt her thoughts.

A moment later, China turned her attention back to Jefe.

"Is it worth it?" she asked him.

"What do you mean?"

"You had all this before," China moved her hand back and forth. "You lost it all when you went to prison and here you are again."

Jefe smiled.

"I do what I do because it makes me happy. It is not for the money I do this. I love it. What am I without this trade of mine? I am nothing. I am not a man of emotions. Love is not something I dream of. I never loved my wife. I don't think she ever loved me. So we are even in that respect. I would never take her over my trade. Now my kids. This is different!"

China waited for him to explain, but it was clear that he was finished.

"So what are we doing tonight? " Jefe asked China.

China told him the usual.

Jefe instructed his worker on what to do. As he waited for his order to be carried out, he spoke to China as it was apparent that she had something on her mind. Jefe needed to know if it was something that would hurt him.

"Señorita China, it bothers me to see you in such a way. Please tell me what bothers you. I wish to help."

"It's Smooth," she said.

"What about Smooth?" Jefe came to the edge of his seat.

"I love him so much, but we want different things and it's pulling us in different directions," China told him, as her eyes began to fill with tears.

Jefe was uncomfortable with China's emotional display, but he tried not to show it. He rose to his feet.

"What is it he wants?" Jefe asked.

China composed herself before speaking.

"He would like to take what money we've already made and go legit."

"What is wrong with that?" Jefe asked.

"It's not what I want."

"And what is it you want?"

"I'm not sure yet, but it doesn't make sense to me to give up the money we're already making just to try and make it back in a different way."

Jefe knew all too well what the young woman was experiencing. It was the same thing he went through with his wife. As a young teenager, Jefe fled his country in search of a better life in the United States. Because of his immigrant status, he was only able to find under-the-table work, which paid him very little. Jefe later found himself in New York because of an old childhood friend. His friend, Ricky, had promised him a good paying job. What made the job great to Jefe was that he wasn't required to do a lot of work. His job was simple. He was required to drop off packages and pick up large amounts of money. Jefe quickly realized that he was selling drugs and someone else was making the profit. Jefe saved enough money to purchase his first kilo of cocaine from Ricky. In no time, Jefe had more clients than he could supply. It was obvious his friend was unable to keep him supplied, so Ricky introduced Jefe to his supplier.

Jefe married his childhood girl who he sent for after he'd made a small fortune. Maria became pregnant almost immediately. After their first child was born, Maria started her campaign to get Jefe to stop selling drugs, but the allure was too strong.

"What you are experiencing is nothing new. Many people in our trade fight these feelings every day. That is because they are not honest with themselves."

China paid close attention as Jefe spoke.

"If you be honest with yourself, Señorita China, you will admit that the money is good, but it is not what makes you a part of this trade."

China smiled.

"You and I are a lot alike, young lady," Jefe said, as he returned her smile.

"My advice to you is to get out now. With every dollar you make, it gets harder to walk away. I've made so much money that I'm trapped forever."

"You don't seem to mind though," China said.

"I've been doing this practically my whole life. I don't know anything else. You have enough money to do whatever you wish and you are certainly young enough."

Jefe's worker came in to inform him that he'd completed his task.

"Are you alert enough to make the trip back?"

"Yes," China said, as she rose to her feet, knowing that was Jefe's way of bringing their meeting to a close.

China walked out after shaking Jefe's hand.

ELEVEN

In the weeks following China's visit to Jefe, she and Smooth had been working hard to get their relationship back on track. The topic of her selling drugs was a touchy one, so they stayed away from it.

"You coming in?" Smooth asked China before turning off the ignition.

"Yeah, why not?" she replied, as she opened the door.

Smooth grabbed the bag from the trunk, before taking China's hand and heading into the back.

Once in the safety deposit box room, Smooth released China's hand in order to fish the key from his pocket. Once opened, Smooth began removing the jewelry from the box and placing it on the counter next to him. After emptying the box, he knelt down, lowered the box to the ground, and began filling it with the contents from the small duffle bag.

"How much is that?" China asked.

"One point five," Smooth looked up at her smiling.

"Look at us, baby. We're putting up millions at 16!"

"You sure you don't want to do what I'm doing?" he asked.

"Maybe some other time."

"There's no point in having that kind of money just lying around the house," Smooth tried again.

"I hear you, baby," was all she said.

Smooth locked the safety deposit box that now held the majority of his money, picked up the bag containing the jewels, and walked out of the bank with China next to him.

Back in the car, the two young lovers listened to Rick Ross, as his music flowed through the speakers.

"What do you feel like doing?" Smooth asked.

"I would like to do some shopping," China smiled.

"Why did I even ask?" Smooth shook his head.

"Baby, I need to get a pair of shoes to match my new outfit I just got for you."

"You got a new outfit for ..." Smooth stopped in mid-sentence as his phone rang.

He answered the phone smiling after seeing that it was Miranda calling.

"I see that you've forgotten about me," Miranda teased.

"Nah, I haven't. I've just been real busy," Smooth was still smiling. China noticed it and made a mental note to find out whom it was he was talking to.

"When will you have time for an old friend?"

"China and I are about to do a little shopping. I'll be free once we're though."

"Give me a call then. I'll be waiting." With that, Miranda hung up.

Smooth placed his phone in the cup holder avoiding China's stare.

Not wanting to start an argument, China placed the phone to the back of her mind. Something was bothering her about the phone call.

Smooth noticed the subtle change in China and decided to question her about it.

"What's wrong, baby?"

China only shook her head.

Smooth removed his phone from the cup holder and held it out to China.

China pushed it away. Seeing that she wouldn't take it out of his hand, Smooth tossed it onto her lap.

"Baby, stop it, please. I don't care who you were talking to," China lied. She placed the phone back in the cup holder.

Smooth decided to let it go.

He entered the parking lot of the mall looking for a parking spot near the door leading to the food court. Even though he hadn't said anything to her, Smooth decided he'd grab something to eat while China shopped.

* * *

Monica sat in the living room watching reruns of *Martin* on the large plasma television. She never tried of the show, and no matter how many times she watched an episode it always made her laugh.

Monica watched as the comedian jumped up and down thinking he'd just won the lotto.

Monica though about what she'd do if she ever won the lottery. Looking around the room, she admitted that her house would look a lot like the one she lived in now with her best friend and Smooth. For the first time, it made her wonder from where they had gotten the money to live as they were.

She got up and began looking around.

Monica stopped just as she was nearing Smooth and China's bedroom. Her heart pounded in her chest as she thought about what she'd say if she were caught in the room. Before going further, she went to her phone and placed a call.

"What's up, girl?" China answered after seeing Miranda's face appears on her screen.

"Nothing. I'm bored," she lied. "Where are you? What time are you coming home?"

"We're at the mall right now. We'll be there as soon as we leave here. You want me to get you something?" China asked.

"Yeah, surprise me!" Monica replied, buying more time to search.

Monica pushed open the bedroom door with confidence, knowing that she had time to look around. She closed the door behind her, making sure to keep the dog out.

Monica opened drawer after drawer, unsure of what she was looking for, but feeling certain she'd know what it was once she found it. Not seeing anything of interest, she moved over to the bed. Monica had trouble lifting the mattress, but was able to just enough to get a look under it. There was nothing there. Before moving to the closet, she looked under the bed. Again, there was nothing. Monica got to her feet and then walked over to the large walk-in closet. Inside, she hit the light switch and looked around. She knew her friend shopped a lot and had nice taste, but what she saw in front of her was enough to open a small high-end boutique. There were several dozen-shoeboxes stacked neatly in the far corner and a dozen more on the top shelf. Monica was amazed at the number of designer clothes that hung from the hangers many of which still held their price tags. She moved along the clothing, randomly checking some of the pockets, looking around the closet. Monica was sure that her girl was up to something.

She checked the shoeboxes in the corner, and then pulled over the small stepladder to check the boxes on the shelf. The first box she picked up was far heavier than any of the boxes she'd picked up in the corner. Monica steadied herself on the ladder, and she then pulled the box from the shelf. Holding it close to her, she pulled off the top. The shock of what she was seeing caused her to drop the box, spilling its contents. She jumped off the ladder; and with trembling hands, she hurried to put the money back inside the box. When the last of it was placed back inside neatly, she stepped back up on the ladder to put the money back. Before stepping back down, Monica checked two more boxes and saw the same thing.

Just as Monica was about to turn off the light, she heard a noise at the bedroom door. She remained quiet weighing her options, and then ran over to the bed and slid under it. The noise at the door continued. This time she heard the distinctive whining of China's dog. He was scratching at the door trying to get in.

Monica hurried over to the door, opening it slowly, so that the dog wouldn't run in. In the hallway now, she shooed the dog away from her. With her heart pounding in her chest, she heard the unmistakable sound of jingling keys. She ran to her room, just as China came through the door with Smooth behind her carrying a handful of bags.

* * *

When Smooth was in the shower, China used the opportunity to go through his phone. She scrolled the call log until she found what she was looking for. She stored the number in her phone, and then placed Smooth's phone back on the nightstand just as it was.

Watching Smooth in the shower from where she sat on the bed, China placed two phone calls, the first was to the number she'd gotten off of Smooth's phone. Before placing the call, she restricted her number.

A female's voice came on the voicemail.

China then placed another call to her private investigator. After giving him Miranda's phone number name, which she'd gotten from the voicemail, she told him exactly what she wanted, which was everything he could find out about Miranda.

With that finished, China went into the kitchen to fix herself something to eat.

Ten minutes later, Smooth emerged from the bedroom with the dog leash in his hand. Seeing the leash, Zorro first ran over to Smooth, bouncing up and down, and then over to the front door where he waited.

"You coming?" he asked China, holding up the leash.

"No" was her quick response.

That's what Smooth was hoping to hear. He headed out the door before she could change her mind.

Smooth opened the door and headed down the hall, where he caught the elevator just as his neighbor, an old white man, was stepping off. The old man stayed clear of the young black man with the pit bull. Smooth wondered if it was the dog or him that the man was trying to get away from.

He decided it didn't matter, as he stepped on the elevator and pressed the button to Miranda's floor.

Smooth stepped off the elevator and was glad he put the leash on Zorro's collar. The dog had spotted a cat just as they entered the hallway and tried to give chase. He whined at the strain of the collar around his neck.

Smooth knocked on Miranda's door and knelt down to pat Zorro as he waited.

Hearing her unlock the door, he rose to his feet.

"Hey," she said, greeting him with a smile when she opened the door.

"What's up?" Smooth replied, as he walked in.

"Who's this?" Miranda asked, kneeling down and pulling Zorro towards her and giving the dog a hug.

After a few minutes of watching her play with the dog, Smooth walked Zorro to the balcony where he left the dog and closed the door.

"Can I get a hug or do I have to be a dog?" Smooth asked with arms open.

"If I was giving all dogs a hug, you'd definitely get one. But I'm only hugging pit bulls today," she shot back.

Smooth smiled and shook his head.

"So what do you have planned for us?" he asked.

"You said you wanted to learn real estate, so I figured we'd get started."

"That's why you wanted me to come up here?"

"Yes. Why do you think I invited you up here?" Miranda inquired, standing there with her hands on her hips and smiling.

Smooth looked at the zipper on her jeans and returned her smile.

"You can get that off your mind. It's not going to happen. She walked over to the bar stools and took a seat, inviting Smooth to sit across from her.

He did.

"Smooth, before we start, let me just say this to you. I l know you can do this. You're mature for your age and you're smart. I know that by some of the choices you've made. You're just the kind of person that would make a good realtor. I don't want to waste my time or your time. If you want this, I'll give it to you."

Smooth raised an eyebrow.

"Stop, boy. I'm for real."

"Yeah, I want it, Miranda."

"Good. Now let's get to it."

* * *

China knocked on Monica's door and waited for her to open it.

"Can we talk?" she asked Monica.

"Yeah, yeah, what's up?" Monica stepped aside so that her friend could enter. She knew what China wanted to tell her.

"It's Smooth," China said, as she climbed onto the bed.

"What about him?"

"I don't know. I think he wants to break up with me."

"Really?" Monica said matter-of-factly.

"What? You don't believe me?"

"Uhhh, no."

"For real, Mo Mo. I even think he's cheating on me."

"Smooth? We're talking about Smooth, right?" Monica asked.

"Duh! I'm serious."

"Why would you think that? That nigga is crazy about you. Trust me, I know."

China wanted to ask Monica what the last words she said were supposed to mean, but she allowed it to go without comment. Monica caught the look China gave her though.

"Don't look at me like that, girl. Don't nobody want Smooth funky behind. I'm just saying I know he's crazy about you because I've been around you two since day one and I know how he feels about you."

"Okay, now. Don't play, girl. Because I'll cut your ass up about my baby," China laughed.

"But for real, why do you think he's cheating on you?"

"He's been acting a little strange lately. Like today, when we got back in, he took a shower and said he was going to walk Zorro.

"Noooo ... a shower before he walked the dog. Girl, I think that nigga got a wife and twins on the side," Monica exclaimed and fell to the bed laughing.

China pushed Monica off her. "You make me sick." She got up and left the room with a smile on her face.

She went to the kitchen to fix herself a sandwich and then she walked over to the couch. She looked at her watch and saw that it was almost three hours since Smooth had left.

Smooth opened the door and watched as Zorro ran over to the couch and jumped on China. She played with the dog, rubbing his tummy for a few minutes before ordering him off the couch.

"Did you cook?" Smooth asked.

"Does it look like I did?"

Smooth ignored China's response.

"Why'd you take so long walking the dog?" she asked.

"Because I didn't want to be here hearing your slick-ass mouth." He walked to the room.

"My slick-ass mouth, nigga. You the one that thinks you're slick. Don't make me fuck you up, Smooth."

"Whatever, China. I'm not in the mood for this. I'm going to sleep."

"Maybe I'll take Zorro for a three hour walk tomorrow."

"Do whatever you want," Smooth said. "That's your dog!"

China wanted to throw something at Smooth as he walked towards their bedroom, but she restrained herself.

China went back to the couch and stared blankly at the television. Smooth was cheating on her and she knew it, everything within her told her so. If Smooth had gone out to walk the dog like he claimed, why was Zorro still so full of energy? If he'd only gone to walk the dog, why wasn't the dog the least bit thirsty? More importantly, if he'd only gone out to walk the dog, why did the dog come back smelling like another woman's perfume? China promised to leave the topic alone until she knew for certain what Smooth was up to.

* * *

China received a call two weeks after hiring the investigator to find out whom the number belonged to that she had given him.

"I'll be back," she said to Smooth and Monica.

"Where are you going?" Monica asked.

"I got to meet Mr. Jameson," China said, as she picked up her handbag from the table and walked out without saying anything to Smooth.

She was sure that he still loved her. Occasionally he'd send her a text message or do something special for her. Every now and then though he'd act as if she wasn't even present. She knew that she wasn't making things easier on either one of them. She kept an attitude. Even when she received his texts, she never replied. She knew that he was cheating on her and she was pissed at him for it.

Monica waited for a while after China left before turning to Smooth.

"What do you feel like eating?" she asked.

He shrugged his shoulders.

Monica got up and went into the kitchen to take out the ingredients to make lasagna. She knew there was no cheese, which is why she opted to make that dish.

"We need cheese," she told Smooth, looking over the rim of the refrigerator door.

"So go get some," he told her, not taking his eyes off the show.

"Come on, Smooth. If I got to cook, you can at least go get the cheese for me to cook with."

"Cook something you got all the ingredients for. I really don't feel like going anywhere."

Monica lowered her head and then let out a silent curse. She'd been trying to get Smooth and China both out of the house at the same time for the past two weeks.

"I want lasagna, and if I can't cook that, I'm not cooking anything," Monica said, coming back into the living room.

"News flash, Monica, you don't cook that good!" Smooth laughed.

"Whatever! I cook better than China," she retorted.

"I agree. And you better be thankful for that; otherwise, you would have had to find yourself a new place."

"I soon will anyway."

"Don't go getting all sensitive on me now, Mo. I already got to deal with China's bipolar-ness. Not you, too."

"My girl ain't crazy. You are!"

"Me? How you figure that?"

"China would do anything for you. And you're too blind to see that. None of this shit means anything to her if she can't share it with you. Both of you muthafuckas are just too stubborn. Believe me, that girl is crazy about you."

"I hear you," was all Smooth said. But his mind was now stuck on China. They had always been behind each other and supporting each other. Smooth wanted things to go back to the way they once were with him and China; and if they couldn't go back, then he

88

figured it was time they went their separate ways.

"I think maybe you should take her out tonight and you two need to talk out your problems. It's obvious you don't want to leave her and she doesn't want to leave you. If that wasn't the case, one of you, or both of you would've already called it quits."

Smooth knew that Monica was speaking the truth. He picked up his phone and made reservations at La Basque. It was China's favorite spot on the beach.

"That wasn't a bad idea, Mo Mo. I think I'll go get that cheese for you."

He picked up his keys and headed to the door.

China was about to insert her key into the keyhole when he opened the door.

"Hey, boo," he said, leaning forward to kiss her.

"Where are you headed? I'd like to talk to you."

"I'm about to grab some cheese from the store for Mo Mo. You want to come?"

"How long will you be?" China asked.

"Ten minutes or so."

"I'll wait until you get back."

With that, Smooth left.

* * *

China locked her bedroom door before she went over to the closet.

Once inside with the light on, she stepped up on the ladder and pulled down several shoeboxes, allowing them to fall from her hands to the floor. She had scheduled an appointment to see Jefe and wanted to get the money ready for the trip.

After counting the money and putting it neatly in her tote bag, China put the boxes back up in their places.

"China," she heard Smooth call her name, as he shook the knob on the door.

China opened the door, holding the tote bag in her opposite hand.

Smooth looked at the bag in her hand.

"I'm going to see Jefe tonight," she explained.

"Tonight? You can't! I made reservations for us at La Basque. After that I thought maybe we'd take a horse and carriage ride and then ..."

"You should've said something to me. I made plans to see Jefe, and you know how he is."

She saw the disappointment in Smooth's face as he fell onto the bed.

"What you want to talk to me about?" he asked.

"I just got back from seeing Mr. Jameson; and before I open this envelope, I want to give you one last chance to tell me yourself."

China walked over to the nightstand and picked up the envelope.

"Tell you what?" Smooth asked.

"Is there something going on between you and Miranda?"

How could he have thought that China wouldn't find out? Now here she was questioning him. He hesitated before answering.

"No, why would you think that?"

China saw the guilt in his eyes.

She reached into the drawer and pulled out the scissors that she always used to cut up the junk mail. Smooth prepared himself for the attack. Instead, China began cutting the envelope in her hand into small pieces.

"Why you doing that?"

"I don't want to find out that you're lying to me. You said there's nothing going on, and I believe you. I'm going to take a shower," she said, once the last piece of paper fell from her hand.

Smooth knew that was her way of inviting him to join her but he wasn't sure at the moment. Instead, he pulled out his phone to cancel the reservations.

"I was thinking maybe we won't have time for the things you had planned after dinner, but we could still have dinner at La Basque."

He smiled and nodded his head.

"And maybe we could do something before dinner," she looked at Smooth seductively.

He undressed and quickly got into the tub behind China. With the water cascading down their bodies, Smooth pulled China tightly to his ɔody, allowing her to feel as he grew with desire for her inch by inch. Cupping her breasts and squeezing her nipples, Smooth lowered his head to place kisses on her neck. Because he was unable to see China's face, he never saw the tears falling from her eyes. China cried ɔecause of how good it felt to be held by the only man she ever loved and she cried because she was exactly where she wanted to be. She reached behind her and found Smooth's dick wedged between her ass cheeks, she leaned forward and slid it into the waiting hole. She ɔlaced her hands on the edge of the tub as Smooth held her by the waist and stroked her from behind. China turned her head to get a look at Smooth's face. What she saw was pure bliss. She knew that Smooth loved her. She turned her head away, allowing the tears to fall freely once again. She wouldn't allow anyone to take him away from her. He belonged to her.

TWELVE

"Let's go, China," Smooth yelled from the living room.

"I'm going to kill you, boy. Stop rushing me. It takes time to look this good," China said, before she spun around for Smooth to get a good look at her.

"You look beautiful, baby," he said.

"You don't look too bad yourself," China reached forward to straighten Smooth's bowtie just a bit.

"Come on, we'll be late," he warned.

China hugged Monica before they left.

Hand in hand, the two young lovers walked through the garage. Smooth opened China's door for her and then placed the tote bag she would take to Jefe in the trunk, before getting behind the wheel.

Once on the road, China lowered the music so that her words would be clearly heard.

"Promise me that we're going to enjoy this night, baby."

Smooth's smile was his only response.

"Promise me," China said.

"I promise," he laughed.

Twenty-five mutes after leaving their place, Smooth and China pulled up to La Basque.

The valet drive opened China's door and then rushed over to Smooth to hand him his ticket.

Inside, the maître d escorted them to their table and placed their menus on the table.

"Your server will be with you shortly," he announced, before departing.

"I love it here," China told Smooth.

"I know. That's why we're here." He reached for her hand and gave it a squeeze.

Smooth's words were simple but true. That's why she loved him so much. He always gave her what she wanted.

The waiter went to their table, took their order, and then left them ое.

"You love me, don't you?"

"Of course I do," he answered.

"Then tell me why you cheated on me?"

Smooth tried to pull his hand from China's, but she held it tightly.

"I'm not going to make a scene unless you make me and I promise we're going to walk out of here just as happy as we did when we walked in. But that's only if you promise not to hurt me again."

Smooth nodded.

"Why did you do it?" she asked again.

"I don't know, baby. In my mind I thought you were going to leave me and it was over with between us."

China nodded. She'd felt that way before also.

"Are you still messing with her?"

Smooth shook his head quickly.

"When was the last time you slept with her?"

Smooth thought for a moment and then answered, "It's been a while."

"So why were you at her place a few days ago?"

"She's teaching me about real estate. I spend a few hours a week with her to learn what I can."

"Not anymore," China said.

Smooth nodded.

The server arrived with their meal. The couple ate in silence, occasionally glancing across the table at each other.

"Come on," Smooth took China's hand after it became obvious that she was finished with her meal. He guided her to the dance floor and pulled her into his arms.

She felt perfect in his embrace, resting her head on his shoulder.

"I love you, China."

"I love you more, Smooth."

* * *

Monica hung up the phone after talking to the dispatcher at the taxi company. The dispatcher told her that a car would be at the address in 15 minutes.

She packed her suitcases and dressed quickly. After getting dressed and placing her luggage near the door, Monica walked boldly down the hallway to the master bedroom and pushed open the door. She was on a mission. As she opened the closet door, Monica could feel her heartbeat in her ear. With sweaty palms, she stepped up on the ladder and retrieved the boxes of money. When she'd finally dumped the money out of the boxes, she opened one of China's suitcases and neatly placed the stacks of money inside. She looked at her watch. The cab would be there in two minutes. She rushed out of the room not bothering to close the door.

On her way out, she patted Zorro's head and then closed the door, locking it behind her. There was a small part of her that felt guilty about what she was doing, but that part was drowned out by the larger part that told her she'd finally be able to live the life she wanted. She made it to the front of the building just as the cab pulled up.

The driver got out to help her with the luggage.

"Where to?" he asked, looking in his rearview mirror at Monica.

"Ah, ah!" It dawned on her that she hadn't planned on where to go once she got the money. "Coconut Grove," she finally said.

Monica settled into her seat for the drive feeling a range of emotions. There was guilt. She felt terrible that she'd just stolen from her best friend. Her best friend and possibly only friend. She wanted to scream at the driver to turn around, but she didn't. She promised herself she'd pay it back after she made a few good investments. Then there was the feeling of loss. She knew that because she'd taken the money, she'd given up on China. She began crying. Already she missed her. China was the only person who had her back for sure. She now also missed Smooth. They argued all the time, but she knew that he was a good dude. She promised to pay him back as well for the money he had given her.

"Where to?" the driver asked again, as he neared Coconut Grove city limits.

"Take me to Tatty's," she ordered.

Tatty's was the only hotel that Monica had ever stayed in. Her first time at the hotel was with her then boyfriend Carlos.

It was her 16th birthday and Carlos had taken her there. They had planned it for months. Carlos cared a lot for her and wanted it to be special when she lost her virginity. She was prepared to go through with it, until she saw the size of Carlos' penis. Monica stared at his large erection and slowly backed up, shaking her head as he approached her. She ran to the bathroom and locked herself in. No amount of coaxing on his part could get her out. Finally, he gave up and left. Monica came out of the bathroom expecting Carlos to enter the room at any given moment. After a few hours, it was clear he was gone for good. She called China and told her to pick her up as soon as she could. Roxy and China went up to the room to get her; but instead of leaving right away, they turned it into a girls' night. Monica told them about what she called her "near-death experience" with Carlos, and they all laughed.

"What his number?" Roxy asked jokingly.

After sharing some of her own stories with China and Monica, Roxy rubbed her stomach. "Let's go get something to eat."

"Let's just order room service," Monica suggested.

They both gave Monica a look as to ask, "Who's going to pay for it?"

"Carlos reserved the room on his dad's credit card."

They all laughed and then called room service.

She'd promised herself that she'd return to the hotel to enjoy it one day. It was a beautiful place. She looked around the lobby as she waited for the elevator. She smiled. That day had finally come.

* * *

"I enjoyed myself, baby. Thank you."

Smooth looked over at China and admired her beauty. He imagined what she'd look like in 30 years. If she looked anything like her mother, he'd be pleased.

"You're welcome," he answered. "Sure you don't want to come up for a few minutes?"

"I would, but we both know that your few minutes always turn into a few hours. As much as I'd like to, baby, I can't. I got to get on the road."

Smooth knew he'd be wasting his time trying to persuade her any further.

"Why don't you come with me?" China asked.

Smooth thought for a moment before answering.

"I'll make you a deal," he finally answered.

China raised an eyebrow.

"I'll go with you if you promise it's your last trip."

It was China's time to be silent.

"It's not like we need the money," Smooth pushed.

"I can't promise you that, baby. But I can promise you that I'm only doing it a few more times."

A few more times could mean three or 350 in Smooth's book. He raised the volume and they both fell silent.

China closed her eyes and allowed herself to think about what their lives would be like without the trips she took to visit Jefe.

She knew things would be better. She knew that's when their problems had started. She thought back to when Smooth was selling small bags of weed. Everything was so much simpler. She finally understood the meaning of "more money, more problems."

She loved Smooth enough to give up everything for him. She never wanted to be without him. Right then, China made a decision. If she ever felt that she was in jeopardy of losing Smooth, she'd give up the game right away.

Smooth pulled up to the front of the building and then put the car in park.

He reached over for China's hand.

"You feeling, okay?" he asked.

She nodded her head.

"China ... I want to ..."

She placed a finger to his lips.

"I know, baby," she said.

"No. Let me say what's on my mind," he said, as he moved her finger away.

"I don't know a time since I met you that I didn't love you. Everything I've ever wanted came wrapped up in this beautiful gift, which is you. I hate myself for breaking our bond and betraying your trust in me. No amount of apologizing in the world could fix things, so I won't waste much time with that. Instead, what I'm going to do is show you with my actions that I'm worthy of your love. I love you, China. And for the little that it's worth, I'm truly sorry."

Smooth wiped away the lone tear that fell down China's cheek.

"Are you finished with her?"

"Yes, baby. I'm finished."

China threw herself into Smooth's arms. For a long moment, she and Smooth held each other's embrace.

"I got to get on the road," China said, extracting herself from his arms.

Again, he wiped China's cheeks.

"Okay, I'm going to let you go. Call me if you need some company."

"I will," she promised.

Smooth opened the door and got out. China crossed over from the passenger seat to the driver's seat.

"You got everything you need?" Smooth asked.

"Yes, baby. Now give me a kiss. I really need to get going."

Smooth bent forward and placed a lingering kiss on China's lips.

"Drive carefully and call me as soon as you get there."

"I will. Now close the door so I can leave," she laughed.

Smooth closed the door and watched as China drove off.

In the elevator, he decided to pay Miranda a final visit. What he had to say to her wasn't something he thought should be said over the phone or via text message. Before going up to her place, Smooth called her to make sure it was okay.

After he spoke to her, he pressed the 24th floor. In the time they had spent together, Smooth had grown fond of Miranda. The sexual attraction was still there, but now he looked at her as a close friend and confidant. She had taken the time to show him things that no one else had, and she had also grown to care a great deal for him.

The elevator stopped on the fifth floor. A middle-aged white man stepped onto the elevator. Smooth looked up from his phone to acknowledge the newcomer and then went back to the text message he was preparing to send China.

He didn't recognize the white man, but the man recognized him right away.

The elevator finally came to a stop. Both men stepped off and headed in opposite directions.

Smooth rang the bell and then waited.

The man turned around and snapped the photo of Smooth, just as Miranda reached out and pulled him inside.

"Smooth stepped into Miranda's living room and watched as she ran back to the spot in front of the television to resume her aerobics workout.

"What's up?" she spoke over the instructor's voice.

"I needed to talk to you about something."

"I'm listening. What's up?"

"It's about China and me."

Still keeping up with the instructor's moves, Miranda finally looked at Smooth.

"Is everything, okay?" she asked.

"Yeah, everything is fine."

"So what's the problem?" Miranda wanted to know.

"Me and you," Smooth motioned to Miranda and himself with his hand.

Miranda stopped the DVD.

"What's the problem with me and you?" she said and then sat next to him on the couch.

Smooth pinched the bridge of his nose. He didn't like having to tell Miranda what he was about to say and he knew she wouldn't like hearing it.

"China and I just got through having a conversation about you and me."

"There is no you and me," Miranda interrupted.

"Let me finish, please. Somehow, she knew that we've been seeing each other. She didn't make a big deal out of it, but she asked me to stop. That's the only way she'll forgive me."

"Did you tell her we stopped seeing each other?"

"We haven't," Smooth dropped his head.

"We have ..." It finally dawned on Miranda. "You mean that she doesn't want us to be friends?"

Smooth nodded his head.

"And?"

"And what?"

"So you're okay with that?" she asked.

"No, I'm not okay with that."

Miranda waited for him to say more, until it became clear he had nothing more to say.

"I guess we're through then," Miranda rose to her feet.

"Please don't be made at me."

"Get out!" Miranda said, barely audible.

"I'm sorry," Smooth said, looking at her.

"GET OUT!"

Smooth took in Miranda one last time before walking out.

* * *

China was about to cross into Georgia when her phone rang.

"What's up, baby?" she answered.

"Nothing. Just calling to check up on you. Where are you?"

"I just entered Georgia."

"That's about where I figured you should be if you're doing the speed limit."

They talked for more than an hour before Smooth began to yawn.

"Go to sleep, baby. Give me a call when you get up in the morning."

"It's already morning," Smooth retorted.

"You know what I mean, boy!"

"All right, all right! I'm going. Call me if you need me to keep you company, or even if you just want to talk."

"I will."

"Drive carefully. I love you, China."

"I love you too, baby. Now get off my phone."

"After the phone call, China continued thinking about Smooth.

He was always so loving and caring towards her.

She turned up the volume just as the words from Sade's *By Your Side* began playing. Because of Smooth, she loved every word of the song. He had dedicated it to her when she had needed to know that someone had her back.

It was in their sixth-grade math class where it all started. The math teacher, Mr. Trickle, called on his students randomly to go up to the blackboard to solve problems. It was his habit to start with the easier problems. He always saved the harder problems for his brighter students. By the time he got to those students, their confidence would be up from seeing their peers solve other problems.

His two brightest students, without a doubt, were China and Shameka. Sometimes he called on China first. This time he called on Shameka.

The class watched and waited as she solved the numeric problem. Finished, she turned to face Mr. Trickle, smiling with all the confidence of a newly crowned homecoming queen.

"Are you finished?" he asked.

"Yes, sir," Shameka responded, as she walked back to her seat.

"Who thinks this answer is correct?" Mr. Trickle asked.

Everyone raised their hands except for China. The teacher noticed her.

"You're all wrong!"

Everyone quickly lowered their hand.

"Since you didn't raise your hand, go up there and solve it," he said and passed the stick of chalk to China.

She rose to her feet, smiled in Shameka's direction, and then walked up to the board with chalk in hand. She erased the marking left by Shameka and then solved the problem just as Mr. Trickle had taught them.

She placed the chalked down.

"Who thinks this is correct?" The teacher asked again.

This time no one raised their hands. Not because they thought it was wrong, it was because China had never gotten a problem wrong. That was why the other student didn't like her. That dislike is the reason they never raised their hands.

"That's the correct answer," the teacher announced to no one's great surprise.

"You may be seated," he told China.

As she walked passed Shameka, the girl stuck her foot out and caused China to stumble. The class erupted in laughter.

Back in her seat, China wrote a short note inviting the girl to a fight after school.

Word spread like wildfire, and everyone waited for the two girls after school, everyone including Smooth.

He tried talking China out of it, but quickly saw that he was wasting his time. Instead, he gave her some pointers.

When Shameka arrived with her girls in tow, she stripped down to a pair of shorts and sports bra.

China walked over to her and got the first punch in. That was also her only punch. Shameka was a bigger girl who fought for all the girls in her clique. But it was China's first fight.

In no time, she was on top of China hitting her in the face. Smooth stopped the fight.

After everyone had left, he used his shirt to clean China's face as best he could. He was extra gentle with her.

"Damn, I got my ass beat," China tried to laugh.

"Yeah you did," Smooth replied.

"You don't have to agree with me."

"It's the truth though. But you know what else is true?"

"What's that?"

"You're still the prettiest girl in this school," he added.

"Yeah right! I'm surprised you didn't walk away with everybody else," China said.

"You trippin', girl! I'll always be by your side."

Later that day, after Smooth had walked her home, he returned to her house with the CD and played the song for her. She fell in love with the song and the boy who dedicated it to her in the same day.

THIRTEEN

Smooth lay in bed listening to Zorro's whining. "What time was it?" he wondered.

He picked up his phone from the nightstand. After seeing how late it was, he pushed himself to a sitting position.

Smooth got out of bed, taking his phone with him, and went to the bathroom and called China.

"Hey baby," China answered.

"Good morning," Smooth said in a groggy voice.

"No, baby, good *afternoon*." Before he could reply, she asked, "Is that my bay I hear whining?"

"Yeah, that's the mutt!" he laughed.

"Watch your mouth! Did you or Mo take him out yet?"

"I didn't. I don't know if Mo did. I'll find out when I get off the phone with you. Where are you?"

"I'm 30 minutes away from Jefe's and I'm tired. I think I'm going to rent a room to get some rest before I head back home," she told Smooth.

"Okay, just make sure you let me know where you're at."

"Yes, sir!"

"I'm serious, baby."

"You know I will, boy! Go take Zorro outside before his bladder bursts."

"Alright! I'll talk to you later."

Smooth hung up with China and turned on the shower.

After getting dressed and finding Zorro's leash, he yelled out to Monica, telling her he was going to walk the dog.

He waited for the elevator. When it finally opened, Miranda was inside talking on her phone and appearing impatient.

She ended the call, knelt down, and played with the dog.

"How are you?" Smooth asked.

There was no response. Miranda's phone rang.

"Did you see it?" she asked the person on the other end.

The person's response made her laugh. She was still laughing when the door opened and she stepped off. Smooth stepped off behind her.

Neither one of them noticed the man walking towards the elevator with his phone in his hand.

Once outside, they both headed in different directions.

Smooth wanted to try again, but he wasn't about to have Miranda continuously dissing him. He accepted the fact that she didn't want anything to do with him and moved on. That's the only way things would work with China anyway.

After scooping up Zorro's waste and dumping it in the trash, Smooth headed over to Tasty's. Tasty's was a small walk-up restaurant with amazing food.

He ordered three burgers, one for him and two for Zorro. When the burgers were ready, he removed the patty from two of them and fed them to the dog. China would go ballistic if she knew he did that. She kept her dog on a strict diet.

After eating and having nothing else to do, Smooth sauntered back home.

Back in the house, he called out for Mo. There was no response.

Getting no response after the third time, he stopped calling.

* * *

Monica sat on the bed looking down on the floor at all of the money in front of her.

There were many thoughts going through her head. She wondered where China and Smooth had gotten so much money. She hadn't counted the money; every time she attempted to, her hands shook uncontrollably. Checking the time on her phone, she decided to get dressed and get out of the room.

Dressed, Monica stared at the money again.

What if the housekeeper came in while she was gone and started going through her stuff, she thought. The thought paralyzed her. She had already lost her best friend. She refused to lose the money as well.

She restacked the money in the suitcase to take it with her.

She paused when she opened the door. What if someone snatched the suitcase or mugged her? The thoughts kept coming.

Finally, Monica remembered the safe. After placing the money inside and locking it, she felt better. She wasn't 100% at ease, but she felt better.

With a stack of money secured in her purse, Monica left the room to do some shopping.

She thought about everywhere Smooth and China would go to avoid those places—those places and places she thought they'd look for her. She had the cab driver take her 30 minutes north into the next county.

"Keep the meter running and be back here in three hours," she told the driver, as he deposited her at the mall's entrance.

Monica handed him several hundred-dollar bills.

"You got it!"

"Monica walked into her first store. She picked up everything her eyes touched or that she liked. For the first time in her life, Monica picked up what she liked, not just what she could afford. She smiled to herself several times. She thought she could get used to this lifestyle quickly.

In no time at all, Monica was weighed down with bags.

She made it outside just as the cab pulled up. The driver got out and rushed over to assist her with the bags.

She fell in the backseat exhausted from the last few hours.

"Where to now?"

"The hotel."

On the way back to the hotel, they passed a row of newspaper stands. She had the driver turn around so that she could get a few. She needed to go through the classifieds section. She needed to find a place to live, and more importantly, she needed to find a car. She would've preferred something new, but she wanted something nondescript and she wanted it quickly.

* * *

China sat in her usual spot while she and Jefe conversed.

She listened half-heartedly as he complained about everything from high gas prices to the lack of loyalty he felt from his employees.

"Nothing is like it was when I started in this business. Back then, there was respect for each other in my trade. Not so any more. Loyalty wasn't something that was for sale. Today it goes to the highest bidder. It makes me sick!"

China had nothing to say. She had none of Jefe's problems. Smooth was the only person that knew what she did. And even if Mo knew, he would never turn against her.

She looked at Jefe as he spoke.

When she had first met him, Jefe appeared vigorous and vital. Now after only several months, he looked as if he'd aged 10 years.

She added the way he looked to what he was saying and made a decision. This trip would be her last.

She listened for a while longer as he continued his rambling.

Finally, he turned to China.

"What can I do for you, my good friend?" he asked.

"Two things." She held up two fingers.

"Tell me."

"First ... this." She slid the bag of money in Jefe's direction.

"I'd like to get my usual."

"Okay."

Jefe called out something in Spanish to his butler, who quickly disappeared.

"Next," he turned back to China.

"How do I say this?" she said out loud.

"You open your mouth and speak."

"Okay, when I left Florida to come up here, I had no plans to make this my last trip. I mean, Smooth has been telling me for a long time now to quit."

Jefe nodded his head remembering the prior conversation he had with China. He listened as she continued.

"He doesn't even know that this is my last trip. I've only just decided it a few minutes ago."

"This is good for you. As I said before, the rules are changing. This business is no good for a young lady. You are wise beyond your years."

China was glad that Jefe was so cool about her getting out. Not that she needed his permission, but it did make her next request a lot easier.

"El Jefe. The second thing I wanted was a special favor."

"Ah, yes, number two. What is it?"

"I'd like you to double my order and allow me to have the funds sent to you when I get back to Florida."

"That's assuming you do get back to Florida," Jefe said.

China had no clue as to how to respond to his last comment. For the first time, she was afraid of him.

He caught the look in her eyes and quickly corrected her thoughts.

"No, no. I'm sorry, my friend. My words did not come out as I intended. What I am saying is that you would like me to give you something you have not paid for. If all goes well, I will get what I always receive. If not, where does that leave me?"

China understood. Jefe wanted more than what she normally paid if he was going to front it to her. That was only right, she reasoned.

"I understand. Just forget I asked. I'll stick with my usual."

"Don't be so easily offended. I did not turn you down. I will not turn you down. You've been good to me. We've been good to each other. I see no reason to stop now."

Jefe yelled out to his butler once more.

"I wish all people were like you and the Negro," Jefe said, referring to Smooth.

China's only response was a smile.

Smooth was going to be ecstatic when China told him she was finished. She planned on telling him as soon as she got back. He might even help her get rid of everything more quickly.

The butler came back into the room, giving Jefe the signal that everything was as he requested.

"Everything is all set for your return trip home."

China rose to her feet and followed Jefe to the door. He spoke to her before opening it.

"Do not regret the decision you made today. It is the best thing for you. Take this," he said, as he handed her a phone number. "This number will stay the same until I die, or until they send me back to prison. But as long as it works, there is a friend on the other end for you. This is my personal number."

China was touched.

The two embraced.

Before China walked out, Jefe kissed her on both cheeks.

"Goodbye, my friend." He waved to China as she left.

* * *

Smooth pulled up in front of Ga Ga's house to find Roxy sitting on the porch.

"What's up, Roxy?"

He took the chair next to her.

"Nothing. You got some money for me?" she asked.

"What you need?" he laughed, while he dug into his pocket.

"Whatever you giving up, nigga."

Roxy was Smooth's older sister, just as much as she was China's. Every time he needed her, she was there for him, just as a big sister should be. He was always happy to break her off.

"Where's Ga Ga?" he wanted to know.

"She just left. She told me to have you give me the money you had for her."

They both laughed at that. Smooth knew that Ga Ga wouldn't accept any money from him or China.

"For real though, where she at? I want to see her before I go."

"Pick up your phone and call her. When she answers, ask her where she is. Then ask her everything else you want to know."

Just like China, Roxy was always sarcastic.

Before putting the money in her pocket, she counted it. She had no idea where Smooth was getting his money from and no desire to find out. She folded the bills and jammed them into her pocket.

"Where China at?" Roxy asked.

"Over there by Korea." He answered with a straight face.

"Who is Korea?"

Smooth couldn't hold it any longer. He burst out laughing. Just then, Roxy realized how dumb she sounded.

"You make me sick!" she smacked him in the head.

"She went to New York," Smooth said, once his laughter subsided.

"For what?"

"Get you some business."

"I don't want to hear that shit. You muthafuckas are my business."

Smooth stayed quiet.

"Is she okay?"

"You tripping, yo. You think I'd be here laughing with you if she wasn't? She went up there to do some shopping."

"Okay," Roxy said and left it that.

Smooth hadn't lied to Roxy, he reasoned. China did go to New York to shop. He just hadn't told her what for.

Just then, Ga Ga pulled into the driveway.

"Don't mention that to Ga Ga," Smooth whispered.

"Duh."

"Hey Ga Ga," Smooth said, as he wrapped her in his arms.

"Hey baby. How are you?"

"I'm good, ma'am."

"And is China? I haven't spoken to her in a few days. Where is she?"

"She's fine," he answered, before he answered her second question Roxy jumped in. "She was just here a few minutes ago. She got tired waiting and said she'd be back later. You know how she is."

"Okay," Ga Ga responded. "If I'm asleep when she comes by, wake me up. I want to see my baby."

With that, Ga Ga walked into the house.

"Why did you just lie to her?" Smooth asked.

"Because she would've been hurt to know you came by to check on her but China didn't. I would never hear the end of it."

"I'm about to wash my car. What are you going to do?"

"The same thing I was doing when your ass got here."

* * *

China felt a sense of relief after having seen Jefe for the last time. She wasn't sure it was her last time seeing him, but she was sure it was her last time in New York. Even that was a lie. She would probably visit New York again ... and soon. However, she was sure she wouldn't be trafficking drugs when she did. She was positive of that.

China was excited to return home. Now things would go back to the way they were before the money entered her and Smooth's lives. Her mind next went to Monica. She hadn't heard from her since she left for dinner the night before with Smooth. That was unlike Monica. If they were apart, no more than four hours ever went by without Monica calling her.

Or had she missed the calls?

She checked her phone quickly. No missed calls from Monica. She decided to call her best friend.

There was no answer. China ended the call when she heard her friend's voicemail.

She thought about sending a text but decided against it. She didn't need to be pulled over the texting while driving. Besides, she knew Mo would call back when she saw the missed call.

She settled in for the long drive ahead of her. To keep herself entertained, China listened to all of her favorite artists' songs—new and old. She was singing along to Beyoncé's *Irreplaceable* when she noticed the SUV in the lane next to her. What caught her eyes was the guy reaching over into the back seat. She saw the car seat but was unable to see the baby it held. The guy was making funny faces and would laugh every so often, almost as if he was making himself laugh with the faces he made. China enjoyed the scene, but what held her attention was that the guy looked just a little older than Smooth. She wondered how Smooth would be with their kids when they finally had them.

She watched as the driver, an older black lady, made her way over to the exit ramp and slowly drifted out of sight.

China was beginning to feel the effects from her lack of sleep.

She decided to stop to get herself a cappuccino and freshen up.

She drove until she came upon a sign that let her know there was a Dunkin Donuts at the next stop.

China ordered then went to the restroom. She went to the last stall and pushed it open. While using the restroom, she heard a female giggling. Being nosy, China leaned forward and looked under the stalls in the direction from where she heard the laughter. She saw a pair of sandals and a pair of sneakers facing each other.

Back outside the restroom, China went to the counter, picked up her order, and left. She looked at her watch. It had been more than six hours since she'd left New York, and already she had made it to North Carolina. She was making good time. Back on the road feeling refreshed, China began singing along to the music until her phone rang.

"Hi baby," she perked up even more.

"What's up, boo? When are you going to get home?"

"I'm on my way. I got a surprise for you, baby?"

"Oh yeah. What'd you get for me?" he asked.

"It's not what I got for you. It's what I did for you."

"I'm waiting on you to tell me."

"You got to guess."

"Oh, let me see. You prayed for me," he laughed.

"No, but one of your prayers was answered."

Smooth was lost. He had no idea what China was talking about now. And he told her as much.

"What are you talking about, boo?"

"I told Jefe it's over. I'm through."

Smooth made no attempt to conceal how happy he was.

China knew the news would make him happy.

"Thank you ... thank you ... thank you!" Smooth repeated over and over.

She wasn't sure if he was thanking her or God.

"I'll tell you the details when I get home."

"Where are you now?" he wanted to know.

"Not far away from South Carolina."

"I'm lying here missing you."

"Don't get me started, boy. I'm about to get back to my driving. When I get to the Florida state line, I'll call you."

"Okay, boo. Be safe."

China was about to hang up when she remembered her friend.

"Why isn't Mo answering her phone?" she asked Smooth.

"Why would I know that?"

"Okay, Mr. Attitude. I love you. Talk to you when I hit Florida."

After hanging up, China plugged her phone into the car charger and tossed it onto the passenger seat.

Refocusing her attention back on the road, China took a moment to think about all of her blessings.

She smiled thinking about Ga Ga and Roxy. Then there was Monica and, of course, Smooth. Those were the people she cared most about. But there were others she cared for, not to mention the money and all of the nice things she was able to purchase. Her life was perfect. She loved the way things were going. When she got rid of what she'd just gotten from Jefe, she'd take both Roxy and Monica to buy new cars.

FOURTEEN

Monica was unable to sleep and wondered how long the dreams would last. She hated the new dreams that plagued her. In one dream, Monica laid down for bed in a room much like the one she was in. Money was piled to the ceiling in neat stacks along every wall. As she lay on the bed, she would watch the money begin to fall. She would put her hands up to stop the money from hitting her in the face, but the stacks of money were so heavy that they'd break her arms and fall on top of her. She would be covered in money and begin to suffocate. Just as she was about to die, she'd wake up breathing hard and out of breath.

She didn't know if she hated that dream more or the dream where she was on a plane looking out the window at the wings made of money. She would stare at the money until one by one the bills would fly away in the wind. After a while, there was nothing left of the wing. The plane would pick up speed as it made its way downward. Monica would always open her eyes just before the point of impact.

She removed the covers and got out of bed. She walked over to the safe and opened it. She looked at the money and wished for the umpteenth time that she hadn't taken it. She wished she could take it back. She knew that wasn't an option. She had seen China calling earlier but refused to answer the call. She knew China well and knew the threats would be plentiful. She was surprised when China hadn't called back.

She turned on the television hoping to find something interesting to watch. After flipping through every channel, she settled on an old Western movie. She hated those. If that didn't put her to sleep, nothing would. Monica had just started yawning when her phone rang. She picked it up and looked at the number on the screen. She accepted the call.

"Hello," she answered, pretending she had just woken up.

"I'm sorry, sweetheart, did I wake you up?" her aunt asked.

"It's okay, auntie. What's up?"

"I just wanted to check on you. I haven't heart from you in more than a week, and I wanted to know that you're okay. I've been meaning to call, but it kept slipping my mind. I know it's late, but I wanted to call before it slipped my mind again."

"I'm fine," Monica assured her aunt.

After Monica's mom had been taken off life support and her stepdad was killed, Donna had stepped up to take in her sibling's children. She had petitioned the courts and received full custody of all three kids. Even though Monica didn't live with her, she was still Donna's responsibility.

Donna and Monica's mother had been best friends all their lives. Monica called her auntie and had no idea that they weren't related. To Monica, she was more than an aunt; she was the best of aunts. Even though she couldn't afford to, she took in her sister's kids at the time of her death, without so much of a second thought.

Thinking of her aunt living in the tiny section-8 apartment with six kids made her feel a lot better about having stolen the money from China. She would do a lot more than simply buy designer clothes like her friend did. Her family needed that money. If that meant no more friendship with China, then so be it.

Her mom was an honest woman who worked hard up until she died. Even though Donna was a good woman, Monica knew she wasn't opposed to quick cash if the risk was minimal.

"When are you coming by for me to take a look at you," Donna asked.

"I have something for you, so I will be by your house tomorrow."

"I'll be home all day, so stop by whenever you get ready."

"Okay, I will."

After hanging up the phone, Monica thought about her brother and sister and felt a pang of guilt. She knew they hated living with their aunt. They always hated visiting her home. Monica had often called to check on them but had only visited them one time since their mother's funeral. She made a silent oath to do better.

She immediately got out of bed and searched for a pen and paper. It was time for her to get serious about what she was going to do with the money. After finding what she was looking for, Monica started her list. On line one she wrote: Take care of family. An hour later, she dropped the pen after her list was finally completed. Everything she needed to do was written on the paper ... everything except purchase a car. She still hadn't gotten one, but she told herself she wouldn't allow the following day to go by without doing so. She turned off the television and finally, feeling much better, fell asleep

* * *

China had the cruise control set to 70 miles per hour, just five miles more than the posted speed limit. It had been more than 30 minutes since she entered the Florida state line, but she held off from calling Smooth. She knew he was asleep. The traffic was light and for that, she was grateful. She hated being on the highway when vehicles sped past her.

She thought about Jefe and what he had said when she asked him for a favor.

"That's assuming you do get back to Florida," he said.

"She hadn't made it all the way home yet, but she was back in Florida. Thinking about Jefe's words sent a chill down her spine. Just as she was thinking about the conversation, her phone rang, startling her. China swerved out of her lane before quickly regaining control of the vehicle. Luckily, there were no cars next to her.

Reaching for her phone that had fallen to the floor from the passenger seat, China swerved again lightly before reaching the phone.

She had missed Smooth's call. It wasn't until she hit the call button to return his call that she noticed the state trooper behind her. China played it cool. She used her signal light to indicate she was able to change lanes. When she did, the trooper also changed lanes. He allowed her to drive for another half mile before he hit his lights. It was China's first time being pulled over; and although she knew it was bound to happen sooner or later, she had no clue as to what to do. Feeling herself begin to panic, she did the only logical thing there was to do.

She pulled to the side of the highway.

After putting the car in park, China placed both her hands on the steering wheel.

The state trooper exited his cruiser and cautiously approached China's vehicle with his hands on his gun. After seeing that she had her hands on the wheel, and that she was the only occupant, he visibly relaxed. He stood close enough to the door where there wouldn't be enough momentum to hurt him if China opened it quickly. He stood with his gun away from her.

"Good morning," the trooper said, tipping his hat to China.

She gave him a nervous smile.

"You got some license, proof of registration, and insurance?" the trooper asked, just before turning to spit tobacco juice from his mouth.

China handed him the items he requested.

"Wait right here."

He went back to his cruiser.

China used her side view mirror to keep her eyes glued to the officer. She thought about calling Smooth but decided against it. She didn't want to make any moves that might give him reason to prolong the stop. She watched as he made his way back to her with the ticket in his hand. He handed it to her.

"What's this for?" she asked, feigning ignorance.

"It's a citation for reckless driving. If I wanted to, I could haul you in and have this pretty little car towed." He pronounced pretty as 'purtay.'

"Thank you for your generosity," she told him.

"Who owns this purtay foreign car you's driving?"

"My boyfriend," China said, and immediately regretted her words.

"Is that right, nah?" the trooper was smiling.

"Can I leave now?"

"He must have a lot of money," he said, ignoring China's question. "He got purtay cars and a purtay little lady. Is he a professional athlete? No, no ... must be one of dem rappers," he answered his own question.

China remained silent. She really wanted to call Smooth now, but was too afraid to reach for the phone.

"You mind stepping out of the car, please?" he asked China, but was already opening the door.

"Why?" she asked.

"Don't question me. Now get out!"

China did as she was told.

Looking at her license and eyeing her from head to toe, he spoke to her again, "It says here that you live in Miami."

China nodded her head.

"Help me understand, little lady. I pull a car over for swerving all over my highway. The driver of the purtay car is a purtay little lady dressed in designer clothes who tells me the car is her boyfriend's car. Do I got that right?"

China remained silent.

"What are you doing in these parts?"

"I'm on my way back from New York. I had to drive my cousins back up there."

The trooper smiled.

"No airports in Miami, huh?"

"It was cheaper to drive, sir," China told him.

"You don't think I believe that nah do ya? I'm sure your boyfriend could afford it. Step to the front of my cruiser, please."

While China stood in front of his car, the trooper looked under her seat. Finding nothing there, he continued to search the vehicle. Finished with the inside, he opened the trunk.

"You can't just search my vehicle," China protested.

He ignored her, opening one of the black bags. When he turned back to China, he was holding a kilo of cocaine in his hand.

"I guess you had no idea this was in there, and you also have no idea what this is," he stated, as he put the package on the hood of his car and ordered China to turn around.

"Please, please, please don't do this! PLEASE!" China yelled.

* * *

Smooth had been calling China's phone for hours with no answer. China was due back any minute. He hated that she wasn't answering.

He hadn't seen Miranda the whole time China had been gone. He couldn't place his finger on it, but there was something nagging him. He had also noticed that China had emptied out all of her boxes. How much was she planning on purchasing from Jefe? She had told him that she'd explain the details to him when she got home. He'd just wait.

The doorbell rang.

Without knowing who was on the other side, Smooth snatched the door open.

He and Miranda stared at each other for a several moments.

"Are you going to invite me in?" she finally asked.

He stepped aside.

Miranda walked inside nodding as she observed the interior design.

"Nice place," she commented.

"Thanks," he stood by the door.

"Is China here?" Miranda asked.

"Why, what's up?" Smooth wanted to know.

"You can relax. It's just a little woman-to-woman chat she and I need to have. It's nothing for you to worry about."

Smooth eyed her suspiciously before answering, "She's not here. I'm waiting for her to get back, and I'm sure she's not going to want to do anything except sleep when she gets in."

It was Miranda's time to eye Smooth.

It was obvious she didn't believe him. He pulled her by the arm to the room that he and China shared.

"Do you believe me now?" he asked, eager to get her out of the apartment. If China were to open the front door at that moment, he and Miranda would be dead meat.

He escorted her back to the front door.

"I miss you, Smooth."

Smooth was surprised to hear the words come from her mouth.

"I miss you, too," he said honestly.

"I can't tell. Why haven't you been by to see me?"

"You know why."

"Oh yeah, that's what I came by to speak to her about."

Smooth gave her a puzzled look.

"The sex was good, but you and I both know that's been over with ..."

"Yeah, but she doesn't know that."

"She will after our lil' woman-to-woman," Miranda said with confidence.

"You might want to swing by later after she gets some rest," Smooth suggested.

"I'll do that," Miranda said, as she opened the door. She extended her arm for a fist bump.

"We cool?" she asked Smooth.

"Yeah, we cool." He bumped fists with her.

He tried calling China again after Miranda had left.

Again, there was no answer.

He walked down the hall to Monica's room and knocked on the door. When she didn't answer, Smooth called her name and slowly turned the doorknob.

Monica had left the closet open. Smooth noticed the empty clothes hangers. He randomly pulled open drawers. They were all empty. He walked out of the room to where his phone was and dialed Monica's number.

"Hello," she answered.

"What's going on, Mo?"

"Isn't it obvious?"

"Come on, Mo. How could you do this to her?" Smooth was pacing back and forth.

"Don't try to make me feel bad, Smooth. What's done is done! There's no turning back. I need this money just like y'all do."

"There's no y'all. That's all China's money, and you know she'd give you anything you fucking asked for."

"I don't have to ask now," Monica told Smooth.

"Look, China don't know about what you did, so undo this, and let's keep it between you and me. If you don't, I swear, Mo, I'll kill you!"

"I'm really scared now," Mo replied, just before she hung up.

"FUCK," Smooth screamed as he threw his phone against the wall.

* * *

Monica hung up the phone and got dressed. She had called the same cab driver who had acted as her personal chauffeur the past few days. There was a lot she needed to do today; and the sooner she got started, the better. She headed over to the safe, opened it, removed a stack of bills, and then locked it back up.

She headed to the lobby to wait for her ride.

While waiting, Monica's thought went back to the brief conversation she just had with Smooth.

She wondered why China had not just called herself. What was the point of having Smooth call? Was it as he said? Did China not know yet?

Knowing China, she could easily believe Smooth. Had China known, she would have called herself. But why wouldn't China know?

Monica was mulling this over when the cab pulled up.

She got in and gave the driver her aunt's address.

"How are you doing today?" the driver asked.

"I'm good, Teddy. How are you?" she returned the question.

The two had started talking on one of the drives back to the hotel. From conversing, Monica had learned that Teddy was a single father of three boys. His ex-wife had walked out on them to travel the country with a young truck driver. The day she left was the last day he had seen or spoken to her. He'd hated her for a long time for what she had done to the boys, yet he was happy for himself.

"What do you have planned for today?" he asked.

"I won't know until I get to my aunt's house," she told him.

For the rest of the ride, they drove in silence.

"Give me a second," she told him, after arriving at Donna's building.

Monica knocked on the door and waited. The noises coming from inside were all familiar to her. She heard the television blasting cartoons, her aunt's voice ordering one of the kids to eat his breakfast, and some crying. She smiled and then tried the door, turning it to see if it was locked. It wasn't. She slowly pushed the door open.

"MO MO!" her little sister ran to her screaming, while wrapping her arms around her waist.

"Hey baby," Donna said, as she walked over to her niece to give he a hug.

The kids were all calling Monica's name. She felt the love. She was with her family.

"Auntie, can I talk to you?" Monica asked, nodding her head towards the room.

"Sure. Michael, keep an eye on your cousins."

In the room, they both sat on the bed next to each other. Monica waited before speaking, deciding on what exactly she would tell her aunt.

"Before you start ..." Donna held up her hand. "Don't tell me nothing if you're not going to tell me everything," she spoke as if reading Monica's mind.

"I did a horrible thing."

"Baby, we can't afford another mouth to feed. Why didn't you use protection?"

Donna was shaking her head.

"No, auntie, I'm not pregnant!" Monica laughed. "It's nothing like that."

"Thank you, Lord!" Donna looked up to the heavens.

"Tell me, what's going on, baby?"

"It's me and China. We haven't been getting along lately," Monica paused.

"That's what friends are, child. One day you're best friends, and the next you're worst enemies. Don't worry about it. Tomorrow you'll be best friends again," she responded, patting the girl's leg.

"I don't think so, Aunt D. Not this time."

"And you said it was you who did wrong to her?" she eyed her niece from the rim of her glasses.

Monica nodded her head.

"Was it Smooth?"

"No!" Monica answered impatiently.

Donna picked up the tone in her voice and addressed it.

"Don't take that tone with me. You told me you wanted to talk to me, but you haven't started talking yet. So don't get an attitude with me for trying to figure out what's wrong with you. I got things to do. Call me when you're ready to talk."

"I'm sorry," Monica said, holding onto her aunt's arm to prevent her from getting up.

She opened her purse and pulled out the stack of money.

"Oh, my Lord! Where did you get so much money from?" Donna asked, as she reached out for it.

"That's actually nothing. I have so much more than that."

"Okay, child. It's time for you to start talking. Tell me everything. And what does this have to do with you and China?"

Donna listened as Monica told her everything that had taken place over the last couple days... ending with her sitting next to her aunt,

"And where did China get the money from?"

Monica shrugged her shoulders.

"Was it worth it?" her aunt wanted to know.

Monica thought for a moment and then answered, "Aunt D. Look at how you're living. You deserve better than this. All she ever did was buy clothes."

"Was it worth it?" she asked again.

Monica nodded. "Yeah, it was," she said.

"That's all that matters. You have to live with what you did. What are your plans?"

"The first thing I want to do is get you out of this place. I'm talking like today."

Donna smiled. She'd dreamed about leaving the projects. Now that it was in front of her, she wasn't sure she could do it.

"I've been here so long, child, I don't think about leaving. This is home."

"Aunt D, this WAS your home. It's time for something better. And I really want to do this for you. You deserve it. Let me do this for you."

"Let me think about it. That's a big decision, child."

"You think about it. You need the space. Take this," Monica said, as she took half the bills and handed them to her aunt.

"I need you to help me get a car," Monica said.

"Okay, when do you want to do that?"

"Right now," Monica laughed.

"Okay, let's me get dressed."

FIFTEEN

China sat handcuffed in the back of the police cruiser watching the police officers talk to each other. She felt as if it was all a bad dream and willed herself to wake up. Try as she might, she couldn't open her eyes to make it all go away.

She started crying again.

She tried breaking free of the handcuffs, only to give up after hurting her wrists. She couldn't believe what was happening to her, but the pain reminded her it was real. The more she fought to get the cuffs off, the tighter they felt on her wrists.

She gave up when the officer opened the door and sat behind the wheel.

He turned to face China.

"I reckon your boyfriend is going to be pretty darn mad. Whatta you think?"

China wanted to kick the smirk right off his face. Her boyfriend. She thought about Smooth.

She knew that Smooth had been calling to find out exactly where she was. What was he thinking now that he wasn't able to reach her?

"Can we talk about this?" China asked.

"Sure we can. What's on your mind, little lady?" The smirk was gone.

China felt a sense of hope serge through her.

"Is there anything I can do to get you to take these cuffs off me?"

"Sure is," the trooper answered.

China noticed the hungry look in his eyes. She hoped he wouldn't proposition her with sex, but if he did, she would have to go through with it. Smooth would never know about it; and if he did find out, he'd have to deal with it.

"What do you have in mind?" she asked him.

"Well for starters, you can tell me where you got all that stuff from, as well as your boyfriend's name and whereabouts would be nice. Whatta ya say to that?" he was smirking again.

China dropped her head.

As they drove to the jail, China noticed the trooper was very upbeat. Was he always like that, or was it the bust he'd just made, she wondered. Whatever it was, she didn't like it.

When they arrived at the jail, the trooper got out and opened the rear door. When China stepped out, she felt the sun shining down on her and took it as a good omen.

Immediately, she perked up.

After being booked for one count of trafficking cocaine, China was given an 11-digit pin number to make her free phone call. She was told that the pin number would give her 10 minutes. She was thankful she would finally be able to talk to Smooth. She would have to wait, however. She was told she wouldn't be able to use the phone until she got to her housing area.

"Follow me," the officer said to China, after tossing her a bedroll.

As they walked towards the cellblock, the officer rattled off a list of rules. China was not paying attention. She only hoped the phone was open when she got there.

They stopped in front of the cellblock to which China was assigned. The officer spoke into the walkie-talkie and a second later, the door opened.

"Good luck," China heard the officer say, just after she stepped in.

She ignored the stares from the other girls and walked straight over to the phone. With the bedroll in one hand, she held the phone between her ear and shoulder as she dialed Smooth's number and then her pin number. Without ringing, his phone went right to voicemail. She was about to leave a message when the phone went dead. China turned to see a heavy-set, baby-faced girl about her height standing behind her. The girl had reached over China to press the dial lever.

Without thinking, China tried to hit the girl with the phone. With surprising agility, the heavy-set girl jumped back. They glared at each other, as several other girls came to stand behind the girl.

"COUNT TIME! COUNT TIME TO YOUR CELLS, LADIES," the officer yelled.

China watched as the girls made their way to their assigned cells.

She didn't move.

"You're in cell one," the office told China.

She looked at the numbers and then walked to cell one. She didn't want to fight the girl, but she wasn't about to let anyone bully or try to intimidate her. That would not happen.

The officer closed the door to the cell after China stepped in. She didn't recognize the girl sitting on the bunk until she looked up.

It was the same baby-faced girl who had hung up the phone.

China dropped her bedroll and attacked her.

* * *

Smooth paced the floor, mad at himself. How had he not known what Monica was up to? And where the hell was China? He looked at his watch. He looked around for his phone and then remembered that he smashed it.

He now needed to get a new one.

Without giving Zorro a second thought, he picked up his keys and walked out.

Before exiting the building, he walked over to the front desk to use the phone. Smooth dialed China's number. There was no answer. He tried to ignore the gut feeling he was beginning to have. He hung up and then called Roxy. He was glad to hear her voice.

"Hey Roxy, I need to talk to you," he said, after she picked up.

"That's what these devices were made for, boy. Talk!"

"Roxy, please not now. Something is going on with China and I don't know what do to."

"Something like what, Smooth?" Roxy was on her feet now.

"I don't know. I got to get a new phone and then I'm coming over there."

"Smooth, you call me and tell me something is wrong with my little sister, and you're worried about a phone! What's going on?"

"I'll talk to you when I get over there," Smooth hung up.

He drove to the phone store a few blocks away from his place. Inside, Smooth gave the sales clerk his phone number along with a story why he needed a replacement.

"And your account security code, sir," she asked.

Smooth had no idea what it was, but he took a guess anyway.

"No, I'm sorry. That's not it!"

Smooth couldn't provide the four digits and therefore was unable to get his old phone number. He thought about driving to the location where he had purchased the phones with China, but he didn't want to waste the trip to the store where he was. He purchased a new phone and left.

After leaving the store, the first thing he did was check his messages. There was nothing new from China. He called her phone, but just as he expected there was no answer. He left her a message. He also sent a text. With nothing to do except wait, he drove over to Ga Ga's house.

Roxy was pacing on the porch smoking a cigarette.

All the time he'd known her, Smooth had only seen Roxy smoke on two separate occasions.

The first was when China had gotten her driver's license and stole her mother's car to go joy riding with Monica and two other friends. The joy riding led to a major accident, sending China and Monica to the hospital. Roxy had smoked cigarette after cigarette while waiting for a ride to the hospital.

The other time was when Roxy was waiting for the results from a pregnancy test and an HIV test she had taken. Roxy had attended a party and become carried away with the alcohol. She had woken the next morning next to Snoop. She didn't remembered sleeping with him. After telling her girlfriend about waking up next to him, she had been urged to get tested. Snoop was rumored to be HIV-positive.

That was more than two years ago.

"Where is she?" Roxy asked.

"I don't know," Smooth walked past her to take a seat on the porch.

"Is anyone here with you?" he asked, looking over his shoulder.

"No," Roxy said, sitting next to Smooth. "What's going on?"

"Roxy, please don't repeat this to anyone. China would kill me if she knew I was telling this even to you."

"Boy, you better tell me what's going on with my sister."

"I don't know, Roxy. I might just be panicking, but my gut feeling
s telling me something ain't right!"

"What do you think is wrong?"

"China and I came across a lot of weed ..." Smooth began. He told
Roxy everything except how they got the weed.

Roxy was speechless when he got through. Smooth had just told
her things that most people would not even be able to imagine. And
one's imagination would be where she would be able to believe his
story came from, if she hadn't seen some of the effects from the
money.

So, she finally asked. "Do you think this Jefe person did
something to her?"

Smooth was shaking his head before Roxy got the words out.

"She was in North Carolina the last time I spoke with her. I think
she got pulled over. She told me she was sleepy. If she didn't get
pulled over, she must've had an accident." Smooth was on his feet
with his hands interlocked on his head. "She won't be able to reach
me. I had to get a new number. If she calls, you make sure you call
me."

"I know. What happened to your other phone?"

Smooth hadn't told Roxy about Monica, but he took the time to
explain what she had done after she asked.

"We talking about the same Mo here?"

"Yeah, now she's MIA. Right now, I'm worried about China.
After I know she's okay, then I'll focus on Monica," Smooth said.

Roxy heard the pain in his voice. She rose to her feet and opened
her arms.

"Come here," she pulled him in, giving him a tight hug.

"Everything is going to be fine."

"I don't know what to do, Roxy. I feel so fucking helpless."

"Don't worry. She's probably home by now," Roxy said, not
really believing her own words. Neither did Smooth.

"There's got to be something I can do. I can't just sit around
twirling my fingers."

"There is something we can do."

"What?" Smooth asked.

"Let me think," Roxy sat back down. "I GOT IT!" she exclaimed and sprung back to her feet with excitement.

Smooth looked on as she pulled out her phone from her pocket.

"Should she have made it home by now?"

Smooth nodded his head.

Roxy continued tapping her screen.

"What are you doing?" Smooth asked, trying to get a look at her screen.

I'm going to get a list of hospitals between Miami and North Carolina, and then call them to see if she was admitted.

"Roxy, there could hundreds of fucking hospitals! That shit could take forever," Smooth retorted, obviously not liking her idea.

"You got a better idea?" she asked him.

"I guess you're right!" he slumped back to the other chair. "Let's do it!"

* * *

China was on the girl's back choking her with one arm and punching her on the side of her face with her free hand. China was having flashbacks of her fight with Shameka and she fought extra hard so she didn't lose another fight.

"Stop, please!" Please stop!" the girl cried, as China continued punching, stopping only when her hand began to hurt.

The girl scooted towards the door, trying to get as far away from China as the small cell would allow her.

Seeing that her opponent was cowering in the corner away from her, China grew more aggressive. She rose to her feet.

"Get up," she ordered.

"What the fuck is wrong with you?"

"What's wrong with me?" China took a step closer towards the girl. "You hung up my phone call and you're asking me what's wrong with me?"

"You're the one who came in here and suck fuck everyone," the girl said.

"I didn't say shit to you muthafuckas! All I did was get on the phone." China noticed that the girl had gotten to her feel and braced herself for at attack. It never came.

"You don't just come in and pick up the phone. And ..."

China listened as the girl, her new cellmate—whose name she earned was Michele, but everyone called Pumpkin—explained things to her.

Pumpkin looked in the mirror at her face and saw that it was slightly swollen.

"I'm sorry about that," China apologized.

"Why did you attack me anyway?"

"Hey, this is my first time, and I thought you're supposed to fuck up the first person that comes at you the wrong way!"

"You've been watching too much TV, girl. It's not like that at all. We all look out for each other in here," Pumpkin told her.

"My bad," China said meekly.

"It's cool. As long as we keep this between us," Pumpkin asked.

"You got it. I know my baby is so worried about me."

"How old is your baby?" Pumpkin wondered.

China laughed, realizing that the girl thought she was talking about a child.

"No, I mean my boyfriend."

"Oh!"

"I was driving back home from New York and now this," China threw up her hands.

"Where is home?" Pumpkin asked.

"Miami."

"I've always wanted to visit Miami," Pumpkin said. "What's it like?"

China was already tired of the girl's questions, but she did her best to hide her frustration.

Instead, she answered the girl, trying her best to answer in a way that wouldn't lead to more questions.

"Well, I'm from Deer Bluff, and it's beautiful there. Every summer the fair comes to town ..."

China pretended she was listening to the girl, occasionally adding a "really" or "nooo" for emphasis. Her mind was on Smooth. She wanted to call him. She needed to call him.

"Clear count, clear count!"

China heard the door to the cells being opened just after the announcement. She walked over to the area and picked up the phone list to add her name just as Pumpkin had told her to do. Just as the officer who had escorted her to the cellblock had told her to do. The officer she hadn't listened to.

After a few minutes had passed and no one got on any of the phones, China began calling names on the list above hers.

"NAY NAY," she yelled.

The girl signaled China to go ahead of her.

After several more names, China finally picked up the phone.

After dialing Smooth's number, she waited for it to ring. Instead, she got his voicemail again.

Smooth was famous for not charging his phone, so China wasn't worried.

Before walking away from the phones, she tried his number again.

She hung up the phone and then walked to her cell.

She sat on the bunk thinking about her current situation and began crying. China prided herself on being strong; but try as she might, she couldn't find the strength within herself. She needed Smooth.

A thought came to China and she headed back to the phone.

After calling off the names on the list, she dialed Roxy's number.

"Hello," Roxy answered.

The tears flowed freely when China heard her sister's voice.

"China, is that you?" Roxy asked, after hearing the sniffles.

"Yeah, yeah, it's me!"

"Thank God, girl. We were worried to death. Where are you?"

After China told her sister where she was, she asked her if she had spoken to Smooth. He'd been next to Roxy the whole time, trying to take the phone out of her hands. Finally, she passed it to him.

"Hey baby," he said to China.

She immediately felt better.

China told Smooth what had happened leading up to her arrest.

She gave him as much information as possible before the phone announced she had one minute remaining.

"Don't worry, baby. I'm on top of things. I'll handle everything."

"I love you, Smooth."

"I love you more. You'll be okay, baby. Just don't drop the soap."

They both laughed.

After the phone call, they both felt better.

She walked back to her cell with a smile on her face. She unrolled the sheets and made up her bunk. China was exhausted. She lay down after she made her bunk to get a few minutes rest. She was asleep as soon as her head touched the pillow.

* * *

Monica felt good about herself. She had given her aunt enough money to put down a hefty down payment on her house and enough money to fully furnish it. Nothing was too good for her aunt. This was a new beginning and Monica wanted everything brand new. Her aunt wouldn't hear of it. Donna allowed her to purchase a new living room set and furnishings for the kids' rooms, but nothing for herself.

Donna and Monica stood next to each other in the furniture store watching as the kids excitedly picked out furniture in the colors they wanted for their rooms.

"I wish you'd get something for yourself, auntie. That'll really make me feel good. It's not like you don't deserve it or we can't afford it."

"Child, stop! You've done more than enough for me. I'm happy with that." Monica left it at that. The money would be there if she ever changed her mind.

"Speaking of money being there," Monica thought to herself, she needed to invest in some up-and-coming companies that all looked promising.

Even though she had only spent a small fraction of her new wealth, she knew she couldn't keep spending without putting it back, or one day it would all be gone. Monica had never had more than a few hundred dollars at a time for herself, but she always managed it well. It was because of those early lessons that Monica was sure she'd never go broke again.

After paying for the furniture and arranging to have it delivered to the new house the following day, Monica dropped off her aunt at the apartment and took the kids shopping for new clothes.

She tried not to think about China, but the more she tried not to, the more thoughts of her entered her mind. She truly missed her best friend.

Again, she wondered why China hadn't called her yet. Monica wished that she would, even if it was only to argue or threaten her. She realized that the more guilt that she felt, the more money she spent.

After having spent all day with her aunt and the kids, she was happy to drop them off after the shopping trip and dinner at McDonalds. She had days left to be out of the hotel. She was eager to get to the peace and quietness of her room.

She kept the radio off in her new car as she drove towards the hotel. Monica had decided to purchase a new car after all. The car she decided on was a mid-size sedan with a decent sticker price and nothing flashy, she thought as she drove through the streets.

China wouldn't take her betrayal lightly. The question that repeated itself over in her mind was "What will China do?" Not only what will she do, but also what was she capable of doing?

Over the past few days, Monica realized that she didn't know Chinas as well as she thought she did. How could she? How had China been able to hide so much money from her? How did make so much money? Was the money China's? Was China's life now in jeopardy because of the missing money? What would she do to get the money back? Would China hurt her? Monica ruled that out. China couldn't hurt a fly. Not the China she knew.

"Time will tell," she mumbled to herself, as she put the car in park.

After opening the safe to make sure the money was still there, Monica took a hot shower and then climbed into bed.

SIXTEEN

Smooth was up before sunrise. There were things he needed to do and he needed to get an early start. The first thing he did was call Roxy. He wanted to let her know what time he'd be picking her up. Because he didn't know when he'd be back home, he decided to take Zorro with him.

He freshened up and then took the dog for a long walk. He wanted the dog to be well spent.

Sitting on the bench in the park, Smooth watched the flow of people headed in every direction as he tossed Zorro's ball. The dog chased it with delight.

Smooth wondered if he would ever be one of the people he looked at. Everyone seemed lifeless like zombies, going about their day on autopilot. These were the people who oiled the wheels of this great country.

He laughed. He'd never been one of them. People like that never got rich. They worked nine-to-five jobs, paid their bills, and hoped their taxes didn't increase. They didn't take chances and they always played it safe. They lacked excitement.

Back at the apartment, he looked at the time. It was 8:45. He dialed Jefe's phone number.

After getting Jefe on the phone and exchanging pleasantries, Smooth got down to the purpose of his call.

"She's in jail," he told Jefe, without saying China's name.

Jefe knew exactly where China was, but he acted as if the news was new to him.

"Say this is not so and you joke with me, my friend."

"I wouldn't joke like that."

"This is most unfortunate. But I should've known all was not well when I did not receive a call from her. Tell me, mi amigo, what can I do? I am at your disposal. China is my friend."

"Right now there's nothing that can be done. She's being held with no bond. All we can do is wait," Smooth told Jefe what he already knew.

"Do you know the circumstances?"

"Not yet," Smooth said, "but I'll let you know when I find out."

"Thank you, my friend."

Wanting to put an end to the call, Smooth stated the main reason he'd called Jefe.

"She told me what was owed, and I'll take care of that today. I just need to know how you wish to receive it."

After making arrangements and promises to keep in touch, Smooth hung up. He called Roxy to let her know that he was on his way.

In no time, he was back out the door walking to this car.

When he got to Ga Ga's house, Roxy was waiting for him. She got in the car quickly and told him to drive off.

"What's up with that?" he wanted to know, as he turned off the street.

"Ga Ga's driving me crazy! She keeps asking me for China, and to get her or you on the phone. She knows something's wrong."

"What are we doing?" Roxy asked.

"Going to the lawyer's office. Did you find out about her visits?"

"Yeah, that's tomorrow," Roxy answered. "I put some money on her books."

"I sure hope this lawyer has something good to say," she added.

"This Jew is the best. I can't tell you how many niggas I've seen him get out of jail. Anyone who got some money will get what they want with him."

The lawyer's name was Timothy Hevralesky. He had an opulent office located in a downtown Miami office building. There were several other practices located in the building, including doctors' offices.

They took the elevator to the fourth floor.

Roxy gave the receptionist her name was told to have a seat.

"Mr. Hevralesky will be with you shortly. Can I get you something to drink?"

They both declined.

Roxy looked around, taking in everything in sight from the plush carpets to the paintings on the walls. Whatever they were, Roxy was sure they were real. A man like this would never ruin his reputation by hanging cheap art in his office.

While they waited, an old couple walked in. The receptionist had they wait just as he did Smooth and Roxy.

The couple who was obviously wealthy sat as far away as possible from them.

A minute after a middle-aged, white lady left the office, Smooth and Roxy were granted permission to go in.

"Ms. Preston," Hevralesky announced, as he rose to his feet and extended a hand to Roxy, before taking a seat and offering one to her.

"Thank you," Roxy said politely.

"My pleasure, my pleasure. Now tell me, what can I do for you?"

The lawyer listened as Roxy told him about China. Smooth noticed that he hadn't taken any notes. Not even China's name. That didn't sit well with him.

Mr. Hevralesky punched several buttons on his keyboard, and then turned his monitor to Roxy and Smooth.

"Is this her?"

They both nodded.

He eyed the single charge: Trafficking in cocaine. No bond.

From experience, he knew the amount had to be significant to warrant a no bond hold. He'd have her out as soon as she went before her judge.

From experience, he also knew he'd be able to charge a hefty price.

"This won't be cheap!" he said frankly. "She has a no bond ..."

"Cut the bullshit!" Smooth spoke for the first time. "How soon can you get her out and how much will it cost?"

For the first time, the lawyer looked at Smooth.

"It's not that easy. First, there's ..."

"Thanks for your time," Smooth said and rose to his feet. "Come on, Roxy."

"I didn't say it couldn't be done. Let me make a call," the lawyer said, as he picked up the phone and punched in a number. Without taking his eyes from Roxy and Smooth, he called out China's name and arrest number to the person the phone.

"Yes, I see. I understand. Can I get something sooner, sweetheart? Very well, I'll be waiting."

After hanging up, he explained things to them. Smooth knew the game all too well.

"Her first appearance is scheduled for next week on Friday. I'm trying to push for something sooner. I'm pretty sure that with her lack of criminal history, I'll be able to get her a bond. How much can the family afford?" he asked.

"You mean how much can we afford to pay you?" Smooth asked.

Before Hevralesky could respond, his phone rang.

While he talked on the phone, Smooth walked out of the room. He took the phone out of the secretary's hand and placed it to his ear, before placing it back on the cradle. He then walked back into the lawyer's office.

"I was just telling Ms. Preston the good news. That was a friend of mine with the Duval County Clerk of Courts. I've managed to get her in front of the judge this coming Monday. It's only a few days earlier than Friday, but I'm sure she'll appreciate it."

"Can you get her out?" Smooth inquired.

"If you mean get her a bond, yes, I can do that."

"How much is your fee?"

"I charge nothing less than $50,000. If the case goes to trial, it'll be an additional $25,000. I can't guarantee you anything as far as results, but I do exceptional work!" Hevralesky smiled, as he leaned back in his chair.

"So, if you're hired, she'll have a bond on Monday," Smooth asked.

"She will," the lawyer responded.

"Give him the money," Smooth ordered Roxy, then he got up and walked out

* * *

Smooth and Roxy's next stop was to the bank to arrange the

money to be sent to Jefe.

Jefe had assured Smooth that the money wasn't something he should concern himself with, but Smooth was glad to do it. He wanted nothing to pull China back into that lifestyle.

Roxy looked over from the passenger seat at Smooth. He had been such an annoying little boy, always at the house like a little puppy behind China. She had grown fond of him over the years. He was far more mature than most boys were at his age. In fact, he was more than most guys twice his age.

At the moment, he was focused on nothing more than China's situation. As Roxy looked at his profile, she got a glimpse of the intense man he was rapidly becoming.

"Is the hotel pet friendly?" he asked, turning to Roxy.

"I don't know. You never told me you were bringing that dog."

"I forgot. Can you check to see if they're pet friendly? If not, we'll have to make reservations someplace else."

Roxy picked up her phone and called the hotel.

"We're good," was all she said, after putting her phone in the cup holder.

"I need a small favor, Roxy."

"What's that?"

"I think it'll be best if we don't tell China when she'll be getting out."

"Why not?"

"Because she'll be overexcited and if all doesn't go well, she'll be overly disappointed. I don't want that."

"I agree," Roxy nodded her head.

Smooth looked at his watch. It was 10:42. Before getting on the highway, he stopped at the gas station to fill up. With a full tank and stops in between, he was sure he'd make it to north Florida in less than five hours. The drive was smooth and uneventful. When he arrived, he shook Roxy's shoulder lightly to wake her up.

"Damn!" Roxy said, as she looked around. "We here already?"

"Come on, Zorro," Smooth ordered the dog, ignoring Roxy's question. Smooth listened as Roxy gave the receptionist her name. He wasn't surprised that she'd only reserved one room. He would've been surprised if she'd reserved two.

Smooth carried their overnight bags in one hand, while holding Zorro's leash in the other.

"This place sure smells pet friendly," Roxy said, turning up her nose.

"We're only here for a night. You can handle it," he laughed.

The room was better than what Roxy expected. And she could no longer smell the animal odor that hung in the hallway.

"I'm showering first," she said, as she took her bag from Smooth's hand.

They were in Jacksonville and had nothing to do until the following day. He unhooked Zorro's leash, pulled out his phone, and sat on the edge of the bed on which he'd be sleeping.

"That shit felt so good," Roxy said, as she exited the bathroom.

Smooth took that as his cue. He stripped down to his boxers and then headed to the shower.

"Roxy was right," he thought, as the water ran down his body.

"YOU HUNGRY?" she yelled through the door.

He turned off the water and then quickly toweled off.

"Let's go out to eat," he said to Roxy, as he dried his hair.

"Okay," she hung up the phone.

* * *

China held up three fingers to her partner. She learned how to play the game on her second day and was already one of the better players on the cellblock.

China's partner was a girl also from Miami. Her name was Tangy. She'd been arrested for fraud charges. Tangy's bond was set at $50,000, but she was unable to bond out. She'd been a part of a group that traveled throughout Florida cashing counterfeit checks at different places. She was arrested coming out of a check-cashing store after the clerk recognized the check to be counterfeit.

While the police blocked her path, the other three girls drove away and left her. She hadn't heard from them since.

China had promised to bond her out as soon as possible.

Tangy liked China. Not because she'd promised to bond her out but because it was obvious to her that China had money. Yet she wasn't stuck up. She was down to earth.

The girls played until they finally lost a game, and then it was time to get up.

"Listen up for your names," the guard announced, after stepping through the door. Tangy and China stepped away from the card table.

"PRESTON!" China was surprised to hear her name called.

She took the large envelope that was handed to her. She noticed that the envelope was from her private investigator and wondered why he'd sent her an envelope.

She walked to her cell and opened it. As far as she could tell, there wasn't much in it. Rather than sticking her hand in it, she dumped the contents onto her bunk.

The pictures fell out face down. She picked them up and looked. China's hands began shaking, and her knees went weak. She could hear her heartbeat.

The first picture was of Smooth dressed as he was the last time she'd seen him. He was standing in front of a door with a female's hand on his wrist. The second picture was of Smooth stepping off the elevator with Zorro. What China noticed more than anything was the female just beside and slightly in front of him. She was clearly enjoying his company from the smile on her face.

China wanted to vomit.

He'd promised her that he wouldn't see her anymore; and as soon as she'd driven away, he had gone to see his side chick.

China stared at the pictures for a while before ripping them to pieces and wishing it was Smooth she was ripping apart.

The thoughts began flooding her mind.

She was determined to stay focused on her legal situation and she tried her best to push Smooth out of her mind.

It was useless. Everything made her think about him.

But why, she wondered. It was obvious that she was the furthest thing from his mind.

She began to cry again.

"You playing, China? It's your ..." Pumpkin stopped talking when she saw the tears rolling down China's cheeks.

"What's wrong?" she asked.

"Nothing," China sniffled, trying to gain control of herself.

"I know it's hard, but trust me, you'll be okay. Everybody's already talking about how much they like you. Don't let it get to you, girl."

Pumpkin had no idea what was bothering China; and rather than telling her, China allowed her to continue assuming what she wanted.

"I'm cool," China wiped her face. "I got to write a letter."

Pumpkin got up and walked to the door. Before walking out, she looked one last time at her cellmate. She smiled and walked out.

Feeling defeated, China sat on her bunk with her head in her hands.

"Mentally, she ticked off everything that was wrong.

She'd just taken a big loss.

She owed Jefe.

Smooth was cheating on her.

She was facing prison time.

She wondered what else could go wrong.

SEVENTEEN

Monica opened her eyes from a long fitful sleep. Through the slits in the blinds, she could see it was a beautiful day. She continued staring beyond the blinds for several minutes. Looking out at the sunny day brightened her mood. She removed the covers from her, walked over to the blinds, and opened them all the way. From where she stood, she was able to view the pool area. She saw couples everywhere she looked. Some were holding hands while they reclined in lounge chairs next to each other. Some were talking, and some were simply taking in the sun. Yet all the faces Monica saw looked happy and relaxed, as if they didn't have a care in the world. Her world was worlds away from theirs.

In her world, there was a safe full of money that she'd stolen from someone who had always had her back. It was money that could get her best friend killed—or worst: herself. It was money she felt better off without. She wished that she could return the money; and had it not been for her family's needs, she would've done just that. At least that's what she told herself. Forcing the thoughts out of her mind, she decided to get dressed and check out of the hotel.

While in the shower, Monica realized that she only had two choices: keep the money or return it. Returning the money was out of the question. With her mind firmly made up, she decided it was time to start doing what she'd always wanted to do.

Saving the safe for last, Monica packed her bags. When she finished packing her clothing, she stood in front of the opened safe.

She wasn't exactly sure why, but the tears were uncontrollable. The sobs racked her body.

She fought to gain control of herself. After she finally did, she began removing the stacks of cash from the safe. Each stack felt like a hundred pounds in her hand.

At the front desk, Monica was informed that she still had a few nights' credit at the hotel.

After answering a barrage of questions about the service and staff of the hotel, she finally left.

Monica was on an emotional rollercoaster and wanted off. She was fed up with feeling happy about having the money and the next moment depressed about China. She told herself that China was no longer her friend and that she'd look at her that way from that moment forward.

Monica drove to her aunt's new house, which was located in a cul de sac in an upper-middle class neighborhood in south Miami. She pulled into the driveway feeling at ease after the long talk she had with herself as she drove to the house.

The money wasn't China's because she didn't work for it. She more than likely stole it from somewhere, so she couldn't be that mad that it was stolen from her.

She used her key to gain access to the house. The house was completely empty. She gave herself a tour, moving from room to room. Monica placed her bags into the closet of the second largest of the five bedrooms.

Monica had carried the bag containing the money into the house with her, but now carried it back to the car as she prepared to leave. She had to do something about the money. She couldn't walk around with the money in a bag forever.

She pulled the investment broker's card from her purse and placed a call to the firm.

After making an appointment, she called her aunt.

Donna was on her way to the house, so that she'd be present when the delivery guys from the furniture company arrived.

Monica thought about having her aunt do one of several things for her, but she decided against any of the ideas. She didn't want to relinquish control of the money to anyone, her aunt included.

Monica's plan was simple. She would invest handsomely in a few large, well-established Fortune 500 companies as well as in several up-and-coming, promising companies.

* * *

"Come on, boy. I want to get something to eat," Roxy told Smooth.

"Chill! I want my baby to be unable to take her eyes off me."

"Yeah, whatever. Can we go now?"

Smooth picked up his keys and headed for the door.

Before driving to the jail, they stopped at a local soul food restaurant where Roxy ordered more food than Smooth thought she'd eat. He ordered a sandwich and a large drink.

Driving to the jail now, he looked at her from the corner of his eyes. He laughed to himself because he knew she wasn't going to eat all of the food.

"This is good stuff," she mumbled with her mouth full.

"Shit!" Smooth said, after making a wrong turn.

He had made the turn on purpose, but he wanted Roxy to think it was as mistake. He was trying to give her time to finish the food.

He was curious.

After finally being able to make a U-turn, Smooth did so. He looked over at the Styrofoam container in Roxy's lap just before she closed it. There was nothing but bones in it.

"You a lil' pig, yo!"

"Whatever, boy. That shit was good. We got to stop there before we leave. Damn!"

Roxy drank some of her soda and then let out a huge belch.

"Pig," Smooth laughed.

They both laughed. It was obvious they didn't mind being around each other. They always cracked jokes on each other, just as they did now.

However, Smooth's attitude darkened as they approached the jail, just as it did each time he got locked up. Today, he felt as if he was locked up again, at least a part of him was—a big part.

Every time he was in juvenile lock-up and China came to visit him, he always noted how good she looked. Now, for the first time, he wondered if he looked good enough for her. He quickly dismissed the thought.

They had far more important issues to discuss.

After signing in to see China, Roxy and Smooth sat down to wait. They were told that she'd be out in 15 minutes. While they waited, they watched several young females step from behind a closed door into the arms of their waiting loved ones.

Every time the door opened, Smooth and Roxy would both look at the door to see if it was China coming out.

Smooth thought about how much things had turned around in the last six months. He was the one visiting China now. Who would have thought? He was excited to see her, but it felt awkward.

He turned to Roxy.

"I need you to do me a favor."

"What's that?" Roxy answered.

"China and I got some real heavy shit to discuss. When I ask you, can you give us some time alone?"

"You really think you had to ask me that?" Roxy said sarcastically.

He shrugged his shoulders.

He was growing impatient waiting. He got up from his seat and began pacing back and forth.

Roxy looked at him as he paced. There was concern etched all upon his face.

Roxy walked over to the check-in counter to find out what was taking China so long.

She was told that China was called for already.

She walked back to her table and pulled Smooth over by the arm as he walked by.

"Sit down," she ordered.

They picked up the deck of cards and started playing.

* * *

"PRESTON, PRESTON. YOU HAVE A VISITOR!" the guard screamed over the intercom.

China didn't tell anyone when her visits were and she was somewhat surprised to hear her name being called.

She had been waiting to confront Smooth about the pictures, and hoped that it was he who came to visit her. She checked her appearance in the mirror and then called Pumpkin.

"What am I supposed to do?" China asked the girl, as she came nto the cell.

"Just wait and ..."

"Preston," the guard called China's name.

"She's going to take you to the visiting area."

China followed the guard out of the housing area to the section designated for visitation. When the guard opened the door, China stepped in. Smooth's back was turned to China when she walked in.

Roxy rose from her seat and ran over to her younger sister, pulling her close into her arms. With tears freely falling, they held each other tightly. Smooth walked over to where they stood and waited for them to release each other. While he waited, he appraised China.

She looked the same, he thought.

Finally, she and Roxy pulled away from each other.

Ignoring her own tear-streaked face, Roxy wiped China's tears away.

"I don't get any love?" Smooth asked, as she stood behind China with his arms open and with a big smile on his face.

China's only response was to glare in his eyes. She turned away from him and followed her sister who was headed to a table. Smooth stood there dumbfounded, staring at China's back and watching as she pulled out the chair next to Roxy.

He brushed her actions off, thinking that she was behaving that way towards him because of her situation.

He took a seat at the table facing China.

After watching Roxy and China talk for 30 minutes, he noticed that she was purposely avoiding looking at him.

He walked around the table and tapped Roxy on the shoulder. After she left, Smooth took her seat.

"You ready to talk to me?" he asked.

There was no response.

He took her hand in his and felt her tense.

"What's going on, boo?"

China heard the pleading in his voice. Her tears began again.

"Why Smooth?"

"Why what?" he asked.

"Wh ..." She was unable to get the words out.

China was facing Smooth, but what she was seeing was Miranda with a huge smile on her face. She was seeing Miranda's hand pulling him into her apartment. But what she saw most clearly was Smooth's betrayal. It was hard for her to look at him.

"Do you have anything you need to tell me?" she asked, just above a whisper.

"Yeah I do, but I need to know how you're holding up in here first."

"I'm fine, Smooth," she pulled her hand away from his. "I'm fine," she repeated.

"Your lawyer's name is Mr. Hevralesky. He assured me that you'll be out of here on Monday."

China listened as Smooth spoke. She listened as he told her about Jefe and then about Monica.

She waited until he got through talking before she said anything.

"So, Monica stole my money, huh?" China asked sarcastically.

"That's what I just told you, right?" Smooth snapped. "You acting like you don't believe what the fuck I'm telling you. I'm losing sleep with you being in this fucking place and now you're brushing me off as if I'm nothing to you. What the fuck have I done wrong? Just tell me that. Please!"

She stared at him for a long time before answering.

"You lied to me."

"Lied to you about what?" he asked.

No response.

"So you're not going to answer me?"

"You lied to me, Smooth. You fucking lied to me!"

"I didn't lie to you and I'm not going to sit here and listen to you make me out to be a liar. You know how to reach me!" With that, he got up and headed toward the door.

"I'll be in the car," he said, as he passed Roxy.

"What's his problem?"

"Fuck Smooth!" China said.

Roxy raised her eyebrow as if to say, "What did you say?"

"How's Ga Ga?" China asked, not wanting to talk about Smooth any further.

Visitation was over, and China made it back to her housing unit, just as the guard announced count time.

She was hoping to make it back in time to make a phone call.

She went to her cell and closed the door.

"How was your visit?" Pumpkin asked, once the lights went out.

"It was okay. Thanks for asking."

For a while, neither girl spoke.

It was China who finally broke the silence.

"Pumpkin, how long have you been in prison?"

"Too long!" the girl answered with a chuckle.

"I know that ..."

"Almost eight months."

"Eight months," China repeated.

"Yeah, it's like that when you don't have a bond."

"Haven't you ever tried getting one?"

"Yeah, I tried. But that didn't do much good. The judge denied me," China fell silent again.

She was thinking about the promise that Smooth claimed the lawyer had made. She knew better. Lawyers didn't promise results. She didn't even think he hired an attorney for her.

China knew what she'd have to do for herself.

* * *

"You don't plan on saying anything to me?" Roxy asked.

"What's there to say?"

"I don't like seeing you like this."

"And I don't like being like this," he retorted.

"So don't be! You and China been here before and you didn't look like this, so why the long face?"

"I don't know," Smooth started. "I never pictured myself with anyone but China. I still don't. I love everything about her; but lately it seems like the more I push, the harder she pulls away. I don't know if I'm what she wants anymore. The crazy thing, Roxy, is that I'd give up everything to go back to the way things were with us before the money came."

"Did you tell her what you just told me?" Roxy asked.

"How can I? Everything I say to her she accuses me of lying. She never told me what I lied about. Everything is 'Smooth, you lied to me!'" Smooth said, mimicking China.

"Did you lie to her?"

"Not you, too, Roxy! That's my partner. I don't lie to her about nothing. Why should I?"

"You shouldn't. And I'm sure you can get her to understand everything you just told me," Roxy said.

"I'm not even sure I care to convince her. I love that girl to death, but it seems like she's got her mind made up about what she wants to do. More power to her."

"Wow! You and China are just alike."

"How's that?" Smooth asked.

"You're both hard-headed as fuck! I don't see how y'all made it this far. But I guess whatever got y'all to this point will get y'all further."

"I hear you," Smooth answered, before turning up the volume.

"I'm not finished talking to you, boy! You don't dismiss me, nigga!" Roxy turned the volume back down.

"And you said me and China are alike?"

"They both laughed.

"I hope you know you didn't make things better by hopping your ass up and walking out on her."

Smooth's only response was to shrug his shoulders.

"SEE, that's the problem! Let me give you some game here. We Preston women are highly sensitive creatures. We love hard and intense. You can have us eating out of the palm of your hands. All we want is attention and respect. We can be a pain in the ass, but that's every woman. Just put up with us when we get a lil' crazy!"

"I hear you," Smooth responded.

Roxy shook her head and then straightened herself in her seat. It was she who turned up the volume this time.

* * *

China thought long and hard about what she was about to do. She got the idea from one of the other girls and decided to go for it. She picked up the phone and dialed Monica's number. China had only been locked up for a few days, but she felt that she had been in jail a lot longer.

"Hello," Monica answered hesitantly, not recognizing the number.

"Hey girl," China was relieved to hear her friend's voice.

"China?" Monica asked.

"Who'd you think it was, the Queen of England," she responded, in her best British accent, before letting out a big laugh.

Monica wasn't sure what she expected from China, but it wasn't what she was getting. After 10 minutes of conversation, she noticed that China hadn't once mentioned the money.

Finally it came.

"And you know what's really fucked, Mo? He tried to get me to believe that you stole my money!"

"Me?" Monica said innocently.

"What hurts so much is that he wouldn't have shit without me. I made that muthafucka, and he wants to leave me for dead! Fuck that nigga! Just like I made him, I'll break him!"

Monica listened as China spoke. What stood out most to her weren't the words she was hearing, but the anger and hurt in the other girl's voice.

China was really hurt.

Monica decided on a course of action.

"How could he say I stole money from you and I didn't even know you had it?"

"Mo Mo, we don't have to go over that because I know it wasn't you. I even received pictures of him and his new bitch. I can't believe this!" China began crying.

"So why are you still in there? How much is your bond?" Monica asked.

"I don't have a bond. And from what I'm learning, I am facing a lot of time."

"What's a lot?"

"Decades!"

Monica couldn't believe what she was hearing.

"I need your help, Mo."

"You know I got you. Just tell me what you need me to do?"

"This is my way out of here, so it's very important you handle it exactly as I tell you. I'm going to contact the prosecutor on my case and do a trade-off; but before I do, I need to know that I'll have what I need. You with me so far?"

"Yeah, I'm with you," Monica lied. She had no idea what China was talking about.

"I need to go by Ga Ga's and check on something for me. It's in my room. Open the big speaker and there should be something taped on the inside. Check it out and let me know if it's still there," China instructed.

"What am I supposed to be looking for?"

"You'll know when you see it. Trust me."

"Why don't you just have Roxy check?" Monica asked, her brain in overdrive wondering if China was setting her up.

"Because I don't want her knowing shit about this."

"Okay," Monica reluctantly responded.

"I'll call you back around 12."

"Okay."

After the phone call, Monica replayed as much of the conversation over in her head as she was able to remember, trying to pick out any inconsistencies on China's part.

There were none.

She had no idea.

She went online to the Duval County inmate information website and typed in China's name. There it was.

Monica was staring at China's mugshot. Even in her mugshot, China was still as pretty as ever, she thought.

She looked at China's charging information and bond amount. The bond amount was as she'd been told. None.

"But who would've thought!" Mo said to herself, after seeing the charge.

China had to be telling the truth. It was all far too elaborate to be a set-up.

Monica got dressed. She had something she needed to check on.

EIGHTEEN

Monica parked just up the street from Ga Ga's house. From where she sat, she was able to watch the house unnoticed. Shortly after parking, she saw Ga Ga get into her car, reverse out of the driveway, and then drive away. She had no way of knowing whether or not Roxy was home. She preferred the house to be empty when she went in.

She waited.

Monica noticed a guy on a bicycle pedaling her way and she stopped him.

"Can I get you to do me a small favor?" she asked him flirtingly.

"The guy stood astride his bike, appraising the young female before him.

"What's that?" he asked.

"Can you knock on that door and tell me if anyone is home?" Monica pointed at the house.

"For $20 I will," he answered.

Monica withdrew a $50 bill from her pocket and ripped it in half.

"You'll get the other half when you get back." She handed a half to him.

Monica watched as he pedaled off to Ga Ga's house.

She waited patiently as he loudly knocked on the door.

Satisfied, she tapped her horn to get his attention. When he came back to where she was parked, Monica handed him the other half of the bill and then waited for him to leave.

She pulled up to the house and hit the horn. She felt confident nobody was home, but she hit the shorn several more times as a precaution. Nobody liked horns honking in front of their house.

Monica got out and grabbed the spare key.

After unlocking the door and stepping inside, she leaned against the door and took in the familiar sights of the house. She knew the house as well as any of the people who lived there. She practically lived there herself.

Urging herself forward, she hurried to China's room.

There were pictures of Smooth and China all over the place. Monica was in several of the photos as well. The pictures brought back a lot of memories. She found the speaker she was looking for and looked it over. She saw that it was one that snap-locked. She went to the kitchen and retrieved a knife. After opening the speaker, she saw what it was that China wanted her to find. It was wrapped in a piece of cloth and duct-taped to the inside of the speaker box.

Now that she was looking at it, she realized that China hadn't given her any further instructions.

Carefully, she detached it from its spot. Monica closed the speaker and then walked out. Before stepping back outside, she peeked through the curtains.

Seeing that the path was clear, she quickly locked up the house and headed back to her car.

A gun.

Why did China want her to pick up a gun, she wondered.

"No," she corrected herself. China never told her to pick up the gun. She only told her to make sure it was still there. She'd make China tell her what was going on before she told her about the gun.

She looked at the clock on her dashboard. It was 10:47. She had just over an hour to wait to hear from China.

To kill the time, she decided to do a lil' shopping. She drove to the mall.

* * *

Smooth sat in his car thinking about China while wishing he wasn't. It was as if she'd invaded every inch of his brain. He loved her just as he always had—of that, he was sure. It was always her he could call on when he found himself in a jam; and now that it was her in the jam, he wanted nothing more than to be the one she called on. The only one.

And he would be. No matter how difficult she tried to make it.

Her bond hearing was coming up in three days and he could hardly wait. The nightmare would finally be over—at least for the time being.

He placed a call to China's lawyer to hear him say one more time that she'd get a bond.

The phone call was brief but effective. Smooth felt reassured.

There was nothing left for him to do except wait.

He went to the bedroom to change his clothes. After putting on his swim trunks, Smooth grabbed his phone and keys, locked up, and went out to the pool.

The pool area had a private entrance and was almost always completely vacant. After gaining entrance, Smooth noticed that there were only three other people using the Olympic-sized pool. He hadn't expected that many people. After all, it was a work day.

He put his keys and phone down and dove in. The water felt warm and refreshing as it washed over him.

Smooth watched as a young white man cut through the water repeatedly, making his way from end to end.

Most people had no idea of the level of physical fitness required to swim several laps in an Olympic-sized pool.

Smooth was impressed not only by the swimmer's distance, but also by the speed in which he covered the distance.

Smooth hadn't realized he'd been smiling when the man got out of the water.

He toweled off and made his way over to Smooth.

"My name is William," he offered his hand.

"What up, William? I'm Smooth," he said, as he shook the hand in front of him.

"Smooth?" The man repeated the name, as if to say that's what your mother named you.

"William?" Smooth repeated in the same manner.

William laughed nervously.

Just then, Miranda entered the pool area with her personal assistance and an uppity-looking, young white couple.

"My assistant will guide you through the remainder of the tour. I normally don't do the tours, but I wanted to give you the tour myself. Unfortunately, some other pressing matter has come up. If you'll excuse me, I'll meet you back at my office once your tour has been completed. I hope you enjoy."

Miranda excused herself with a head nod and smile. She walked over to where Smooth and his new acquaintance sat talking. He didn't notice her until she was a few feet away.

"Hello, Mr. Johnson ... Mr. Blanc," Miranda spoke first, hoping Smooth would pick up on her formalness.

"Ms. Burkley," Smooth said.

"Hi, Ms. Burkley, how are you?" William asked.

"I'm fine. Thank you for asking," she replied, never taking her eyes off Smooth.

"Mr. Johnson, I've left several messages personally on your contact numbers and have yet to receive a return call. There are a few important issues we need to go over. Can you please contact me at your earliest convenience?" she asked, as she thrust her card in his face.

He took the card from between her index and middle finger.

"I got a ..."

"At your earliest convenience," she silenced him.

"I'll do that. At my earliest."

"I hope I haven't interrupted anything important, and I beg your forgiveness if I did. You gentlemen have a pleasant day." With that, she walked away. She could feel their eyes on her as she did.

"That was amazing. Holy shit!"

"What are you talking about?" Smooth asked.

"Are you kidding me? She practically threw herself at you."

"You trippin'!"

"I know women bro and that one wants you bad."

"I don't think so. I have a faulty dishwasher that I'm sure she just wants to get replaced as badly as I do."

"I see where the name comes from now," William laughed.

* * *

China tapped her feet impatiently as she waited for one of the phones to become free.

What seemed like hours to China was only seven minutes in reality.

She picked up the first open phone and dialed Monica's number.

"Come on, come on, come on!" she repeated, as she waited for Monica to pick up.

"Hello," she finally answered.

"Talk to me," China said, wasting no time.

"Was it wrapped in plastic?"

China released the breath she hadn't realized she'd been holding. There was only one way for Monica to know that.

"Thanks, Mo Mo! I know I can always count on you. Now I can do what I got to do."

"What's going on, China?"

"Don't worry, Mo. It's nothing. I just ..."

"Nothing my ass! You're going to tell me what's going on, or I'm not going to be a part of this!"

"I don't think you really want to know. Just trust me on this," China answered.

Trust.

Monica almost laughed out loud. Her own actions in the last several days made her know that nobody was to be trusted. She never thought she'd steal anything from China.

"You can say what you want; but unless you tell me what's going on, you're going to have to get Roxy to do this."

She saw that Monica wasn't budging.

"Somebody I know did something with that and I'm going to use that to get out of this place."

Monica went silent for a second, thinking about what she had just heard.

"You there?" China asked.

"Yeah."

Monica didn't have to think hard. She knew exactly who that someone was. She also had a plan forming in her head. She just needed to know what was done with the gun.

"China, how could you put me in a position like this? You got me in possession of a dirty burner. I don't need to know who, but you better tell me right now what this shit was use for."

China pinched the bridge of her nose. She wanted to strangle Monica.

"What do you mean you're in possession of it? I never told you to move that shit. Just put it back and ..."

"I'm not going back there. Just tell me what you need me to do. I'm your girl and you know I got your back, but you always keep me in the blind on everything. That ain't right, China."

She knew Monica was right, but she couldn't help it. She was naturally a secretive person. China lived by the code: If you're not a part of it, you don't need to know about it.

She rationalized with herself about her next move. She was asking for Monica's help, so technically she was a part of it now.

She explained to Monica what was done with the gun.

Monica pretended indifference for the last few minutes of her phone call with China, but she was screaming with excitement on the inside.

Her biggest fear was one day having to confront China. She wasn't so worried about that anymore. She wasn't worried about China's boy either. She had what she needed to keep him in line now.

She couldn't believe how easily it all came together for her.

She had no intention of doing what China had asked her to do. For the first time in her life, she had the ups on China, and she admitted to herself that it felt good.

"So that was where the money came from?"

Monica would never have guessed it, even though the signs were right there, especially the car that Smooth got shortly after it happened. Now of all places the gun could have ended up, it was in her hands. She knew the first thing she had to do was secure the gun. Monica drove home without so much as a second thought as to what her plans would do to China.

* * *

After hanging up the phone with Monica, China dialed the number to the D.A.'s office. After being transferred and placed on hold multiple times, she was finally told that the district attorney assigned to her case was out to lunch.

She refused to offer to leave a message and said that she'd try back later.

With nothing left to do, she called her sister.

"Hello," Roxy answered.

"Hey hoochie! What's up?"

"Un-uh, baby girl. It's Ms. Hoochie. Get it right!"

They both laughed.

"What's going on?" China asked.

"Nothing much. I'm hanging out with Kimmy."

China heard the girl in the background telling her to keep her head up.

"Why haven't you called Smooth yet?" Roxy got serious with her sister.

"What am I calling for him for?"

"Are you serious? That boy is doing everything he possibly can to get you out of that place, and making it as easy as he can for you while you're there. Who do you think put money on your books? Smooth, that's who!" Roxy answered her own question."

"Yeah, my money," China said inaudibly.

"What?"

"I said it was my money."

"How was it your money when that trifling bitch stole all of your shit?" Roxy asked.

"I see he told you that bullshit too, huh? Don't worry, I got something for his ass."

"Bullshit. No, he didn't tell me any bullshit. He told me the truth. I know it's the truth. Too bad you don't believe him."

"What makes you so sure he's telling the truth?" China asked.

"The bitch packed all of her shit and moved out. Why would he pay the dude the money that you owed? Why would he hire the best attorney in Miami for you? Use your head, girl!"

"So he really did get an attorney for me?" China asked the question but already knew the answer.

"Not just any attorney either! Now ask me how I know that's the truth?"

China remained silent.

"Now you're ass don't want to talk. I'll tell you how I know anyway. I'm the one that paid the lawyer. Why would he go through all that for you?"

Something wasn't right.

She knew what Roxy was telling her was the truth, but that truth still didn't explain the pictures. The pictures that she also knew were telling her the truth.

Still, Roxy had a point. Why do all that?

China wanted to think. After hanging up with Roxy, she headed to her cell for whatever privacy she was able to get.

Everything was a jumble for her.

Smooth paid for her lawyer.

Smooth paid Jefe.

Smooth made sure they were there to visit her.

Smooth's actions were not that of a disloyal person. But there were the pictures. Smooth's face was there clear as day. No matter what Roxy said in his favor, it was obvious he'd betrayed her. Again.

It was obvious what he'd keep doing if she allowed him to.

Then there was Monica.

What about her? China wondered.

She couldn't point to a single reason that led her to believe what Smooth had told Roxy about Monica stealing the money—what Smooth told her.

She cautioned herself not to think with her heart. Her head told her clearly who was responsible.

Yes, Smooth had done a lot for her in the past several days, but it was all done with her own money.

China left the cell and went back to the phone.

She was told that the D.A. was still at lunch.

She hung up the phone in frustration.

She needed to reach the D.A. before her court date to ensure that she did, in fact, receive bond.

NINETEEN

Smooth and Roxy sat in the front row of seats in the courtroom waiting for China to come in. Before entering the courtroom, he'd spoken to her attorney and was told that he'd be there in 15 minutes.

Every time the door opened, Smooth looked behind him to see who had entered. He knew the lawyer was on the way, so he urged himself not to get anxious. Still, he was unable to control himself.

The door opened again and finally Mr. Hevralesky entered. His eyes scanned the pews until they found who he was looking for.

He made his way over to them.

"Good morning," he said, as he placed his briefcase on the floor next to his feet.

"Good morning," Roxy replied.

Smooth simply nodded.

"Don't worry about anything. The judge presiding over her case is Judge Bach. He and I were roommates in college. But more importantly, we spoke by phone last night." He winked at them.

They both caught his drift.

"Let me ask a question before Ms. Preston goes before the judge," Hevralesky said, as he looked down at them in their seats.

They waited.

"How much bond can you afford? I'm only asking because I don't want to get a bond that the family can't afford."

"So why don't you get it as low as you can?" Smooth asked.

Hevralesky smiled, unbuttoned his coat, and then took a seat next to them.

"Let me explain how this works. First of all, on a charge like this, the defendant normally sits in jail until the trial date. That's not going to happen here. You don't need to know why. But since she's not going to sit in jail, the D.A. is going to raise holy hell. The way we quiet him is by simply not insulting him. You simply don't give a no-bond defendant a low bond. It has to be plausible. You get me?"

"Yeah, I get you," Smooth answered.

"So what's plausible?" he asked the lawyer.

"One hundred thousand."

Smooth simply nodded.

With that, the lawyer got to his feet and went over to where the docket was kept.

China was scheduled to be in the first group brought to the courtroom.

Rather than going back over to Smooth and Roxy, the lawyer went over and chatted with the clerk. It wasn't long before she was laughing and touching his arm affectionately.

Judge Bach entered the courtroom.

After calling the court to order, the clerk sat back down.

"Mr. Hevralesky, who do I owe the pleasure of having you grace my courtroom?" the judged asked.

"The pleasure is all mine, your honor," Hevralesky said, picking up the docket. "Page one, Ms. Preston, your honor."

Judge Bach peered through the glasses perched atop his nose, looking at China's charges.

It was all for show. He knew every piece of pertinent information related to her case.

The door where the defendants entered the courtroom opened and a guard led a line of handcuffed people to their assigned area.

China waved in Smooth and Roxy's direction with both hands.

They both waved back at her.

Smooth noticed China rolling her eyes. He could only shake his head.

"Your honor, Ms. Preston is present," Hevralesky pointed in the general direction of the defendants. He had caught Smooth and Roxy's waving at one of the defendants.

"What is the matter before the court?" the judge asked.

"Your honor, Ms. Preston was arrested for the first time on ...," he said, as he flipped through several pages looking for the date of her arrest. "She was arrested on November 2 for trafficking cocaine and has been held on a no-bond charge. I'm requesting bond to be set in this case, your honor."

The judge turned to the D.A.

"Any objections?"

"Yes, your honor. The state strongly opposes any bond being set in this case. Counsel for the defendant would like to put forth the notion that the defendant is a juvenile, but the 60 kilos of cocaine she was caught with is very disturbing. Again, we strongly oppose."

The judge listened to the D.A. and Hevralesky went back and forth trying to persuade him to side with their argument.

"I've listened to both sides and I've reached a compromise. I'm going to set a bond in this case. Counsel, what do you think is an appropriate amount?"

At this, Hevralesky smiled.

"Ten thousand, your honor," the lawyer answered.

"And the state."

"Two hundred thousand, your honor."

"Bond is set in the amount of $200,000."

"Thank you, your honor," both lawyers said.

Hevralesky shook the other lawyer's hand, and he then walked over to where Roxy and Smooth sat.

After exchanging a few words with them, he gave the judge one last look and walked out.

* * *

After leaving the courtroom, Roxy and Smooth drove over to the bail bondsman's office. The bondsman's name was Duwan Raymond. Smooth had initially gone to Speedy's bail bonds in Miami, but he was directed to the office in Jacksonville.

After arriving they were asked to have a seat. Mr. Raymond would be with them shortly.

After waiting several minutes, a short, heavy-set black man with far too much jewelry and not enough hair emerged from the rest room, wiping his hands with a paper towel.

"You got visitors," the secretary said, pointing to the two.

"How's it going?" Raymond said, extending his hand to Smooth.

"I'm good," Smooth shook his meaty hand.

"What can I do for you?"

"I got someone I need bonded out."

"Sure, sure, sure. Bonds we can do. If you needed a hit man, you came to the wrong place, but bonds we can do. That's our business. That's what we do!" he laughed at his own joke.

Smooth and Roxy looked at each other.

"Come on over here," he guided them to his desk.

"Who're we springing today?" he asked, as he sat in front of his computer.

Roxy slid the paper with China's name and jail number across the desk to him.

They watched as he typed in the information and then slowly shook his head.

"What?" Smooth said.

"She don't have a bond," he replied and turned the computer screen toward them.

"Yes, she does! Her bond is $200,000!" Smooth said with a lot of emotion.

"$200,000?" the bondsman asked. "Hang on!" He picked up the phone to call over to the courthouse. He didn't want to miss the 10 percent fee.

Smooth got to his feet. He needed to move around.

What did he mean she didn't have a bond?

He walked back to the desk as the bondsman hung up the phone.

"What's up?" he asked.

"Everything's A-Okay. Just a slight oversight. The clerk forgot to enter the information into the computer. It should be done now."

He re-entered the information into the computer and turned the screen around to them again.

There it was.

"Do you folks know how it goes?"

"No," Smooth quickly answered.

Mr. Raymond's eyes told him he didn't believe him, but he explained it anyway.

"So," Roxy said, after he got through explaining, "... if we decide to use you, we got to pay you $20,000?"

"That's me or anybody else. This is a risky business, sister."

"How long will it take for her to get out of there once her bond is paid?" Roxy wanted to know.

"The information goes into the jail system right away. It's up to them after that. They normally take anywhere from 45 minutes to 8 hours."

"Just pay the man, Roxy. The longer you sit here asking questions, the longer she'll have to sit in jail."

Roxy pulled out two $10,000 stacks from her handbag and slid them to Mr. Raymond.

He fanned through the money and then called his security over.

"Count this and get me a receipt," he ordered.

"That takes care of that. There's still the matter of collateral."

"You need to call Speedy's," was Smooth's only reply.

With that, the bondsman filled out the paperwork. After everything was completed, he had Roxy sign, and he gave her a copy of the receipt. He thanked them for their business and then watched as they left.

After leaving the bonds office, they drove back over to the jail. There was nothing left to do but wait. They both hoped the wait would be closer to 45 minutes rather than 8 hours.

* * *

It had been almost 48 hours since Monica last spoke to China. The conversation had taken a turn for the worst when China demanded her to replace the gun back in the speaker.

Monica had told her that she'd taken the money. She knew that sooner or later she'd find out any way. Why delay the inevitable?

Besides, Monica had all the security she needed. China had told her out of her own mouth that she was facing 20 years and possibly a lot more. With any luck, Monica hoped that was what she'd get.

As for Smooth, she was certain he'd stay in his place. She had nothing to worry about, she told herself.

She lay across her bed reading the *Investor's Business Daily* on her iPad. She had invested a large amount of money into four companies and checked them obsessively. She was proud of her choices. So far, the companies she selected had made her more than $17,000. And that was in three days of trading.

Maybe she would make enough to give China a loan, she laughed to herself. NOT!

Just then her phone rang. It was China.

"Yesss," she answered in a teasing tone.

"What's going on, Monica?" China asked.

"Oh, just looking at my investments," Monica continued with the tone.

"What investment would that be?"

"Nothing you'd understand. So tell me, why are you calling me?"

China knew exactly what Monica expected from her, so she approached her from a different angle.

"Do you remember how we first met?" China asked her.

"Yeah."

"I was the one that befriended you when everybody shot spitballs at you. If I'm correct, I'm the one who made them stop."

"You were."

"Do you remember when your mom lost her job and couldn't afford school clothes for you? Do you remember who gave you half of everything she'd gotten that year?"

"You did."

"Do you remember who you came to when your mom passed away?"

"I remember," Monica's voice was low.

"Not one time, Mo, have you ever needed me and I wasn't there for you. Not one time! And the first chance you got, you do me like this? Fuck the money. I don't even care about that part as much as you might think I do. What's hurting me so much is that it's you who did it to me. I didn't even hurt this much when I thought it was Smooth who did it to me. But come to find out, it was you! My best friend, my sister, one of the few people I'd give my life for."

Monica remained quiet.

"Even if you were to offer me back that money, I wouldn't accept it. That money was worth the lesson you taught me. I just have one request Mo, and you'll never have to worry about me every again."

"And what's that?" she asked.

"The item I asked you to check on. The item I asked you to check on ... not touch. Can I please have it back?" China pleaded.

"As bad as I want to, I can't do that!"

"You can't or won't?"

"Whatever suits you best. Just know that I'm not!" Monica stated firmly.

"Just tell me why!"

"I'm not telling you anything. As a matter of fact, lose my number!" With that, she ended the call.

She replayed everything China had just said.

China was right. She always had Monica's back. Even the times when she hadn't said anything to China, she'd found out somehow and was still there for Monica.

She had kept China on the phone for more than six hours when Gary had dumped her. It took someone who really cared about her to listen to her sobbing for that long.

China had always been a friend to her, but she was never a friend to China. It was about time China recognized that. She figured she was doing China a favor in the long run.

* * *

"So ...," Roxy turned in her seat to face Smooth, as they waited in the parking lot for China to get released. "How much money do you guys still have?"

"Touch your nose, Rox. Touch your nose."

"I'm not trying to be all up in your business. I'm just asking because I want to ask a favor of you."

"How much the outfit cost, Roxy?" Smooth went into his pocket.

"No, Smooth. I'm thinking about opening a restaurant," she said.

He leaned over and placed the back of his hand on her forehead.

"You okay?" he asked.

"Yeah, I'm okay," she slapped his hand away laughing. "I got to start planning my future. Ga Ga keeps stressing this college shit, and I'm not feeling it. Maybe if I can start a successful business, she'll lay off."

"Maybe."

"She might even give me the money she saved for me."

"Yeah right!" Smooth said.

"A girl can wish."

"I'll tell you what. If China's okay with it, I'm okay with it."

"Noooo ... you're putting me off on the Wicked Witch of the West?" she laughed. She laughed because she knew she'd get the money.

China wouldn't turn her down.

"Speaking of the Wicked Witch ...," Monica pointed.

Smooth got out and waited by the hood of his car as China made her way towards him.

With tears in her eyes, she ran to him. She needed to feel the familiar strength of his arms wrapped around her. She needed him to know she loved him. She needed him to know how sorry she was. But more than anything, she needed his forgiveness.

Smooth swept her off her feet and held her tightly. They were in another world. It was Roxy who brought them back.

"Hey jailbird."

China broke free from Smooth's embrace to give her sister a hug.

"Y'all got something for me to eat?" China asked.

She was wearing the same dress she had worn when they went to dinner the night she went to see Jefe, and Smooth noticed that it didn't fit her frame as tightly as it did when he last saw her.

"What do you want to eat?" he asked her.

"You" was her response.

"I do not want to hear that shit," Roxy said, and got in the car.

Smooth pulled China in his arms once more and kissed her deeply.

Pangs of pleasure and guilt were what she felt at the moment.

"So what do you feel like eating?" he asked again, once they were in the car.

"I don't care. Surprise me."

"Let's go to the spot we went to last time we were up here," Roxy said from the backseat.

Nobody objected.

"Look at this girl," Roxy grabbed a handful of China's hair.

"I know. It's a mess," China agreed.

Having China next to him, Smooth felt like he'd been awoken from a nightmare.

He continuously stole glances of her. He needed to know that she was really there.

They reached for each other's hand at the same time.

Smooth parked near the door of the restaurant.

Roxy got out and went inside. Shortly afterward, she came out with a menu.

"Whatta you want?" she handed the menu to her sister.

After taking their orders, she headed back inside.

China looked at Smooth and asked herself how she could have ever doubted him. He had proven his love for her countless times. She realized that she'd betrayed him just as much as Monica had betrayed her.

How could she ever tell him what she'd done? How could he ever forgive her? She couldn't tell him, yet she knew she had to.

She opened her mouth to speak, but nothing came out.

"What's on your mind?" Smooth asked.

"You."

"What about me?" he was all smiles.

"Why did you lie to me?"

"Please don't start this shit again, China. If you're going to tell me that I lied to you, at least tell me what you think I lied about."

"Okay," China said. "Answer this, what did you do that night after I dropped you off?"

Smooth thought for a moment. Then it came to him ... Miranda. There was no way for China to know though. But she had to. Why else would she be asking?

He hadn't done anything wrong, so he had no reason to lie.

"After you dropped me off, I went up to Miranda's place," he told her.

"So you did lie to me. You told me you wouldn't see her anymore."

"Technically, I guess I did lie to you, but I only went up there to tell her I wouldn't be coming around anymore. Nothing happened."

China wasn't sure if she believed him.

"And that was the last time you saw her?" China wanted to catch him in a lie, even though she wasn't sure what she'd do if she did.

"Actually no. I bumped into her on the elevator and she came to our crib one morning and ..."

"S'cuse me? She came where?"

"She said she wanted to have a woman to woman chat with you."

China looked at Smooth for an explanation.

He shrugged his shoulders.

What he just told her explained the pictures she had received.

She accepted what he told her.

"I need to get out of this dress."

"And I can't wait to get you out of it."

"Is that right?" she leaned over to kiss him.

"Hello," Roxy was standing by China's door with both hands filled with food.

China got out and opened the door for her.

China ate most of her food without once looking up to see where they were driving.

After finishing her meal, she reclined her seat.

Before Smooth got on I-95, China was fast asleep.

TWENTY

"Thank you for everything, baby," China told Smooth, as she stripped down to her underwear.

"I'm just doing my job."

China smiled at him and then walked into the bathroom, leaving the door open. Smooth wanted desperately to go in behind her, but he resisted the urge.

There'd be time for that later.

He wanted her dressed and ready to go as soon as possible. Roxy had made him promise to have China at Ga Ga's house as soon as she got home from work. He wanted her there before Ga Ga got home.

He walked out of the room.

Even though the case still loomed over her head, Smooth was happy to have her home.

He picked up his phone and called Speedy. He thanked the bondsman for his help in getting China out without the collateral. Ga Ga was the only person he knew that had collateral to put up. Of course they could have paid the full bond amount, but Smooth wondered what that would have looked like.

Not long after he ended the call, China came out of the bedroom dressed and ready to go.

She had towel-dried her hair and put it in a ponytail.

Smooth looked at her with an appraising eye. She passed his inspection.

"Come on." He took her hand and led her out the door.

China chatted non-stop and Smooth listened. He listened, even though he knew there was something else on her mind. He knew her too well. He knew her well enough not to push her. So he waited.

"I thought about so much while I was in that place," she said.

"I bet you did," he laughed.

"For real. There's so much sadness in there. I see why you didn't want to continue doing that shit."

"It's more than that, boo," Smooth told her. "There are two sides o everything. When you decide to take chances that can lead you to prison, you got to always remind yourself not only of what you can gain but also of what you can lose. I'm always going to be by your side, you know that. But I got to say I wish you would've listened to me. Besides, what Mo stole ... look at how much we can still lose."

China liked that he said "we." But that was part of why she loved him so deeply. With him, it was always "we."

She wanted to defend her decision to continue, but didn't because she knew he was right.

Roxy was sitting on the porch when they got there.

"Hey jailbird," she greeted China.

"Stop calling me that," China demanded.

"Touchy, touchy!" Roxy laughed.

"For real. What if Ga Ga hears you saying that shit?" she asked.

"I know. I'm just fucking with you, girl."

"I'm going to Banga's crib. I'm not trying to be here when Ga Ga gets here. Call me when you ready."

Before he turned to leave, they heard Ga Ga's car pull into the driveway.

"Too late," Roxy started laughing.

"Damn!"

"Well, if it isn't the prodigal daughter."

"Hey Ga Ga," China was all smiles as she walked in her mother's arms.

"Hi Ga Ga," Smooth said.

"... and the prodigal son. Come here, boy," she said, giving Smooth a half-hug while still holding on to her daughter.

Roxy opened the door and they all walked inside.

"Where have you been for the last week, young lady?"

With downcast eyes, China answered her mother.

"Busy with school work," she lied.

"School work, huh?"

"S'cuse me y'all," Smooth attempted to walk out.

"Sit your tail right back in that seat," Ga Ga ordered.

"Now who's going to tell me what's going on?" the old lady

asked.

They looked at each other, but no one spoke up.

"Why do you think something's going on?" China inquired.

"Let me ask the questions, lil' girl."

Roxy knew this wouldn't turn out well.

"Where have you been for the last week, young lady?" her mother asked again.

Both girls knew from experience that their mother always knew the answer when she asked a question more than once.

Still, China held her ground. She could tell her mother the truth.

"I told you, Ga Ga."

"You told me a lie is what you told me. What about you, Roxy? Where has your sister been?"

Roxy looked between her mother and sister, and she was unsure of which way to go.

"I have nothing to do with this," she said, as she stood to her feet and walked out.

After Roxy was gone, Ga Ga turned to her youngest daughter.

"Let me tell you something, child. I had you 16 years ago and there ain't nothing I don't know about you. You or that thing that just walked out of here," Ga Ga pointed at the door.

"I know good and well where you spent the last week. Mamas got a way of knowing when their babies need them. It's a mother's intuition. I've relied on my intuition to raise y'all this far, and it ain't let me down not once. It told me something was going with you. I get at least one call from your every day, and all of a sudden I don't hear from my baby. And when I get to calling you, all I ever get is your voicemail. Girls your age live for their phones. So I asked myself what's the reason you wouldn't have your phone turned on. You was either dead or in jail."

China remained quiet as Smooth shifted in his seat.

"I'll be outside," he attempted a second escape, but sat back down when he caught the look that Ga Ga gave him.

"I don't know what's going on, but I don't like it. My blood pressure is through the roof and I need answers before I worry myself into a stroke."

China hated when her mother used her health against her. This time was different though, because she saw that her mother looked worn out.

"Ga Ga, me and ..." Smooth started to speak, but was cut short by China.

'Ga Ga, I was in jail." She gave Smooth a dirty look. "But I'm fine now. I'm sorry that I had you worried; but I promise you, you don't have to worry any more. That'll never happen again."

"But why were you in jail?" Ga Ga persisted.

"It's nothing. Please don't worry about it."

"And you promise it's over with?"

"Yes ma'am, it's over with."

"Okay, if you promise," she rose to her feet and headed to her bedroom.

* * *

Monica walked to the back of the house with the metal box in one hand and a shovel in the other. What she was about to do wouldn't take long at all.

After selecting a spot, she placed the box on the ground and began digging. She looked around at the neighbors' windows each time before she shoved the shovel into the dirt in her aunt's garden. After digging a deep enough hole, Monica got down on her knees and lowered the box into the hole.

As quickly as she could, she refilled the hole and then patted the dirt, trying to blend it in with the untouched soil around it.

She stepped back to look at her work. The spot wasn't invisible, but she was confident it would easily go unnoticed.

Her aunt paid no attention to the garden. They had only been in the house a few days, but her aunt had yet to do any gardening. She wasn't worried about the metal box being uncovered.

She returned the shovel to the garage and then returned inside. Her aunt was still sitting in the same spot in front of the television watching her soap operas.

Monica walked to the kitchen to wash her hands. While she

washed her hands, she noticed how easily her aunt could have seen her had she walked into the kitchen while she was outside.

She laughed to herself, finished washing her hands, and then walked to her bedroom.

She toyed with the idea of calling Smooth to tell him what China did, but decided against it.

She had given him fair warning. She had told him that China didn't deserved him. Now he would see why.

She actually liked Smooth, she told herself. She had no intention of hurting him and hoped that China wouldn't force her hand.

Just then, a thought came to her.

She wondered how much money Smooth still had and how much he'd be willing to pay for the gun. She mulled it over for a while.

It all fit perfectly. If she got all of Smooth's money, she could relocate somewhere out of state. With no money, Smooth would be unable to reach her.

There was only one problem. She had no idea how much he had. She couldn't ask for too much or too little. She decided to hold the gun as security for her safety.

She picked up her iPad and logged onto her favorite website. While she logged in, Monica realized just how isolated she had been since she stole the money. She was reluctant to go anywhere on the off chance that she'd run into Smooth. She had security now, but even with that, she still preferred staying out of sight.

Monica first checked on her investments and then scanned the site for news on up-and-comers. She jotted down the names of several of them and then went about researching them.

While she researched, Donna continued to watch the television. But Monica had no clue as to what was really going on in her aunt's mind. Her mind was locked on the metal box she saw her niece burying in the back yard

Whatever it was, it was something her niece didn't want anyone to find.

Her aunt wondered what it could be. She wasn't a nosy person, but she did like to know what was going on around her. She made a mental note to look inside the box.

* * *

Smooth and China lay on their bed next to each other, going over the events of the past week. Eventually, the conversation turned to Monica.

"Where do you think she is?" he asked.

"I have no idea. Shit, with all the money she has, she could be anywhere."

"Why would she do that to you?"

"Money makes people do foul shit."

"How did she even know you had that money in the closet?"

"Baby, how hard was that to find? She was here alone and maybe decided to snoop around. She came across it and the rest is history."

Smooth sensed that China was already fed up with his questions so he dropped it.

"Something has been bothering me and I need to get it off my chest. I won't ask you not to get mad, because there's no way that you won't get mad," China told him, as she slowly eased away from him.

After hearing what China said, Smooth said up on the bed.

As if he knew what was coming, Zorro ran out of the room.

"Don't look at me like that!" she told him, trying to force a smile.

Smooth was unpredictable when he got mad. She knew what was coming. She just hoped it wasn't too bad.

"China, if you have something to say, just say it," his voice was low.

He spoke as if he was extremely tired.

"Do you remember the day we robbed Boss?" she started.

"How could I forget? But why are you bringing that up? I thought we agreed never to speak about that again."

"I know, but ..."

"But nothing! We leave the past where it is," he said.

"Please listen to me."

Smooth sensed something important was coming, so he remained silent.

"Do you remember what you did the night you dropped me off?"

He thought for a second but had no idea what she was talking about.

"Why don't you tell me," he said, thinking she was talking about another female.

"The night you dropped me off ..." China started, "I had you give me the gun that you used to kill Boss."

"You were supposed to get rid of it, I remember."

China stayed quiet too long.

"What did you do with it?" Smooth asked.

China remained quiet.

"What did you do with it?" he asked again, only louder this time.

"I didn't know what to do with it, so I wrapped it up and hid it inside the speakers in my room," she cried, tears streaming down her cheek.

"So what's the big deal if it's in the speaker? We'll get it the next time we go over and get rid of it."

China was already shaking her head as he spoke.

"We can't!" she told him. "It's not there anymore."

"Whatta you mean it's not there? Where is it?"

Her sobs racked her body.

Smooth didn't see what the big deal was. Even if the gun was missing from the speaker and his prints were on it, that didn't prove anything. He could have held the gun at any time.

Of course, he still didn't like the idea of the murder weapon out there with his prints on it.

"I thought it was you, Smooth. I thought it was you!" China said in between sobs.

"What was me?" Smooth was confused.

She got herself together, and then told him what she had done.

"I got the pictures while I was in jail," she showed the photos to him.

Smooth looked at himself in the pictures and wondered who had taken them.

"I told you I went to see ..."

"I know," China cut him off.

"What does this have to do with the gun?"

"When I got the pictures, it was right after you had told me that Monica had stolen all of my money. Then I spoke with her and she was so convincing. I thought it was you."

"You thought I would steal from you?" he looked at China as if he didn't recognize her.

"I thought you had abandoned me when I needed you most. So I told Monica to go get the gun."

Smooth had his hands wrapped around her throat before she was able to finish her statement.

"Why did you tell her to get it?" he asked between clenched teeth.

"I can't brea ..."

"Why did you tell her to get it, China?" he asked again.

He saw that she was having trouble breathing, but he still held her by the throat.

She pried his fingers loose and managed to break free. Smooth walked around the bed and grabbed her by the hair.

He was no longer looking at China. The person he saw in front of him was a total stranger. The China he knew would never try to hurt him, even if it meant hurting herself.

Still holding her hair, Smooth punched her as hard as he could in the face and watched as she fell to the floor.

"Shame on you, China!" he screamed, as he kicked her in the ribs.

"All this time I was your scapegoat, huh?" He kicked her again.

"You wanted me to go to prison, stupid bitch!" he spat on her and began walking out.

"Smooth, please don't ..."

"He grabbed his keys and walked out, not bothering to look back.

* * *

Smooth dialed Monica's number and then crossed his fingers. He was sure he'd be able to get her to see his point of view, if only she would answer.

He was glad Monica had put all the numbers on to his phone.

"Hello," Monica answered.

"What's up, Mo?"

"Smooth?"

"Yeah, it's me!"

"I didn't recognize the number. You better be glad I answered."

"I am."

Monica thought he sounded happy indeed.

"Why you so happy I answered?" she wanted to know.

"Because I need to talk to you."

"About?"

"Listen, Mo. Me and China ain't together no more. So what you and her got going on don't have nothing to do with me!"

"Is that right?" Monica didn't believe a word he said, but stayed on the phone because she had nothing else to do at the moment.

"That's right," Smooth said.

"So why are you calling to tell me this?" she asked, even though she already knew the answer.

"You got something that belongs to me and I need it."

"And what might that be?" Monica teased.

"Come on, Mo, let's not play this game. You know what I'm talking about."

Monica laughed.

"I'll make you a deal, Smooth."

"I'm listening," he replied.

"You leave me alone, and I'll leave you alone. You don't have anything to worry about from me."

"I believe you, but you know I can't have that hanging over my head."

"I don't think you have much of a choice," she laughed.

The call wasn't going like he expected.

"How much do you want for it?" he tried another angle.

"How much can I get for it?"

"$100,000!"

Monica laughed again.

"That's all your freedom is worth to you? If that's the case, you might as well let me give you that much to be my slave," Monica was enjoying herself.

"Let me make this easy for you, honey. I got money. You know that I do. But I don't have security. Would you go skydiving without a parachute?"

"Not unless I was trying to get myself killed!" Smooth answered.

"I'm not trying to die, Smooth. I got a reason to life. In fact, I got millions of reasons."

"You leave me no choice then."

With that Smooth ended the call.

TWENTY ONE

China sat on the bed clutching the pillow as she cried. The pain she felt was unbearable, not physically, but emotionally. She loved Smooth with all of her heart and it was tearing her apart to know that he had left the way he did. It hurt even more to know that she deserved it. At that moment, she hated Monica and wanted her dead more than anything. She had to find her.

China picked up the phone and called her private investigator.

After telling him what she needed, she hung up and slowly made her way to the bathroom.

She looked at her face in the mirror. She gently touched her bruised eye and winced. She also felt soreness in her ribs where Smooth had kicked her, but that pain was bearable.

China had never been a person to sit back and wait for things to happen.

She dressed, called a taxi, and went downstairs to wait.

"China?"

She turned around and saw Miranda walking towards her.

She was thankful for the oversized dark glasses she wore, but silently cursed under her breath.

"Hi," China said.

"How are you?" Miranda asked.

"I'm fine. How are you?"

"I'm good. Thanks for asking. I know this may be a little awkward, but I'd like to talk to you about Smooth."

Tears sprang from China's eyes at the mention of his name.

"Do you want to talk about it?" Miranda took China by the hand.

"You wouldn't understand. Trust me."

Miranda laughed.

"We all got a past, and I'm sure what you're dealing with right now is nothing I haven't been through."

"I'll take your word for it."

China couldn't place a finger on it, but she liked Miranda.

"Let's go to my office."

"I can't. I'm waiting for a taxi. I'll come by and see you when I get back."

Before Miranda could answer, a blue and white cab pulled up.

"I'll see you later," China said, as she got in the back seat.

China gave the driver Ga Ga's address.

On the way to Ga Ga's house, she sat in the back seat in deep thought. Only a week earlier, her life seemed so perfect. She wanted for nothing. Now, only a week later, she had nothing. Nor did she care. All she wanted was for things to go back to what they used to be with her and Smooth. She pulled out her phone and dialed his number again. She knew he wouldn't answer.

She was right.

The diver discreetly stole glances of the attractive lady in his back seat. He wondered the reason for the sadness he saw in her face.

He reached the address she had given him. After paying the fare, China got out and was thankful that Roxy was there.

"Hey, y'all," she said to Roxy and Meka.

"Hey," they responded in unison.

"I need to talk to you," China pulled Roxy into the house.

"What's up, sis?" she asked China, once they were out of earshot of Meka.

"Smooth left me."

"Y'all are always going through something. It ain't never been a big deal. Why you acting like it's a big deal now?"

China removed her glasses.

Roxy let out a gasp.

"Who the fuck did that to you?" Roxy was pissed.

"I deserved this and a lot more, Rox. I showed you this to say I think it's really over this time," China said, as she put her glasses back on.

"So Smooth did this?"

"Would you just listen?" China ordered.

"Talk!" Roxy folded her arms and began tapping her feet.

China told her sister about what she had planned to do and how Monica now had the pistol.

Roxy had stopped tapping and now stared at her younger sister as if she had two heads.

"How could you do something so fucking stupid, China? What the fuck is wrong with you?" Roxy exploded.

"I thought ..."

"You thought shit! You didn't think. If you did, you would have seen that he had your back since day one."

"I don't need to feel any worse," China sunk to the couch.

"I can't believe you would do something so stupid. So where is Smooth now?"

"I don't know. He just left and hasn't answered his phone since," China began sniffling.

Roxy picked up the phone and called Smooth.

"What's up, Roxy?" he answered.

"Hey Smooth," she looked at China, who jumped to her feet.

"Where are you?" Roxy asked him.

"Just driving around."

Roxy noticed that he sounded extremely depressed.

"China told me what happened," she told him.

"She did, huh? Did she tell you why?"

"She told me that, too. I just want you to know I'm not mad at you."

"Thanks, sis. I just can't figure out why she would do some shit like that to me."

Smooth and Roxy talked for several more minutes before disconnecting the call.

"Where is he?" China asked.

"He ain't nowhere!"

"What does that mean?"

"He's just driving around, China."

"I know what I did was fucked up, sis, but it sounds like you're on

Smooth's side."

She received a dirty look from Roxy.

"That's your problem right there, girl. In your eyes, it's a his side and your side. But in his eyes, if it hurts you, it hurts him. We would've never did that to you. So no, lil' sis, I'm not on his side, but I'm damn sure ain't against him! And you should never have been either, especially for that no good trifling hoe."

"I know. Ohhhhh, I want to get my hands on that bitch so bad."

"So what's your plan to get Smooth's life out of her hands?" Roxy asked.

"I got to find her first, and I need to buy a gun. I'm going to fucking kill that bitch!"

"Where are you going to buy a gun?"

"I have no clue," China told her.

Roxy went to her room and came back with a shiny silver pistol wrapped in white cloth and handed it to China.

"Two things," Roxy held up two fingers. "You didn't get that from me and don't ever bring it back to me."

China placed the gun in her purse and zipped it closed.

"Thank you, sis. This never happened."

Both girls laughed.

"What are you doing with a gun anyway?" China asked.

"You ain't the only one that got a little thug in you. It runs in the family, girl."

"I don't know what you talking about," China laughed again.

"China, let me say this to you, Smooth really loves you. If I were you, I'd do whatever it takes to get him back. He's a good young nigga and he'll only get better with time. He's the one any woman would be smart to marry."

China listened as Roxy explained to her what type of man Smooth was.

She knew her sister was right about Smooth, just as she was about Boss. She agreed with Roxy.

She'd do whatever it took to get him back.

* * *

Nick Ferro, the private investigator China hired for all the investigative work she needed, dialed a number and then waited.

"Hey there LeeAnne, I got one for you."

He waited for a moment and then spelled out Monica's full name.

After being placed on hold, Nick picked up the pen and jotted down the information.

"Thank you, LeeAnne."

He typed the address into his navigation system and followed the address. After arriving at the location, he drove passed the house and parked a few houses down where he'd be able to keep the house under surveillance.

After more than three hours of waiting, he was surprised to find a white family exiting the car, with the kids running to the front door. It was obvious they lived there. He looked at the address on the paper and on the house. They matched.

He pulled up in front of the house just before the middle-aged man walked inside.

Nick got out.

He explained that he was with the Department of Children and Family and he needed to investigate a report of abuse on a Monica White. He looked at the paper with Monica's information on it.

"There's no one that lives here by that name."

Just as Nick had suspected.

"How long have you been living here?" he asked.

"Just over three months," the man answered.

"I'm sure it must've been the family that lived here prior to your family. Our caseload is so heavy that we can't get out to investigate reports of abuse in a timely manner. I apologize for the inconvenience."

Nick got back in his car and drove away.

He could justify his rates to China as long as he produced results.

He headed back to his office. He needed more information on Monica. She was going to be more difficult than he first thought. But he was Nick Ferro, and he always found his subject.

He called his contact at the post office, but was told he was unavailable. Nick would have to call back another time.

The next call he placed was to China.

"Let's hear it," she answered the phone.

"Up until a few months ago, she lived at ..." He looked at the paper and gave her the address. "Now, I have run my normal checks. Because of her age, I'm sure she doesn't have any credit cards or property in her name. So that brings me to the purpose of this call."

"Which is?"

"What can you tell me about her ... about the people closest to her? Give me your best guess as to where she might've run off to. Does she have any family out of state that she can turn to?"

China thought for a moment.

"She has two younger brothers, Marvin and Marlin. The only family member I know of is her Aunt Donna ... Donica Kelly. Oh shit!"

"I take it you have something for me," Nick said.

"Her brothers are in her aunt's care. Or at least they were up until I got arrested. So all you've got to do is find her aunt."

"That's what I need, kiddo. C'ya."

Nick hung up the phone and went to work.

It was always easier to find adults. Underage subjects were usually what he called ghosts, because it was hard to find any trace of them.

"Let's see what Donica Kelly turns up?" he asked himself.

* * *

Smooth sat on Miranda's couch in deep thought.

It was obvious to her that he had plenty on his mind and she suspected that China had a lot to do with it.

"Have you eaten?" she asked.

He shook his head.

"What would you like to eat?"

"Whatever you cook," he told her.

"Cook? You better look through these menus," she handed him a stack of menus from different restaurants in the area that delivered.

He half-heartedly picked a Chinese restaurant and handed it back to her.

After placing the order, she took a seat on the recliner and looked at him for a long while.

"Do you want to talk about it?" she finally asked.

"Talk about what?"

"The pain you're going through right now."

"It's that obvious, huh?" Smooth said.

"Yeah, added with the fact that I saw China today and she was a hot mess herself, and she began crying when I mentioned your name."

Smooth laughed. He'd never heard anyone describe China as a hot mess.

"Why did she start crying?" he wanted to know.

Miranda recognized the hurt lover in Smooth. He needed to know that she was in pain as well.

"Whatever you guys are going through is hurting her just like it's hurting you," Miranda replied, knowing he needed to hear those words.

"China really hurt me, Miranda. I never thought she'd ..."

"Thought that she'd what? Cheat on you? Maybe she thought the same thing about you, Smooth. But she forgave you."

Smooth shook his head.

"It's not another nigga. She betrayed me, and I can't ..."

"You men are all the same. You betrayed her. Betrayal is betrayal. She forgave you, so it's only right for you to forgive her."

"It's not that easy, Miranda. You don't understand."

"Then make me understand," she said.

"Let's just drop it."

"Fine by me."

They sat in silence until the doorbell rang.

Miranda paid the deliveryman and then ordered Smooth over to the dining table.

After placing their food on plates, the two dug in.

Smooth's mind was on China, and Miranda's mind was on him.

Occasionally, she looked up from her food to steal a glance at Smooth.

"You know," she dropped her fork with a loud clank on to her plate. "I'm glad I put a stop to us when I did."

"I was that bad, huh?"

"No, actually you were real good," Miranda replied and felt a ingle between her legs when she thought about their sex.

"I'm just glad that I didn't allow myself to get pulled in any deeper."

"How deep did you get pulled in?" Smooth asked, holding Miranda's stare.

"Not as deep as you and China are with each other. Not even close."

"How should I take that?" he asked her.

"Anyway you want," she returned.

Smooth returned his attention to his food.

"All I'm saying is this, Smooth. I'm glad I was able to get a hold of myself, because you're obviously something special. I saw the hurt n China's face earlier and it's obvious to me that she loves you. Looking at her made me regret my actions with you. You guys love each other. I know it just as well as you know it. But let me share something with you that you may not know."

Smooth lowered his fork again to show Miranda that he was paying attention.

"When you love someone you accept them as they are, not as the person you think they'll be or the person you believe you can make them out to be. You share in their pain and you delight in their pleasure. You always want what's best for them, even when that's not what's best for you. Love is forgiving. If you love this girl like you say you do, and then find a way to forgive her. Forgive her because you love her, but also forgive her because you know she'd forgive you, Smooth."

"Would she?" Smooth asked himself.

For the first time when it came to China, he wasn't sure.

"Can I ask you something?" Miranda inquired.

"Ask me anything you want."

"Are you ready to walk away from her?"

Smooth didn't answer. He wasn't sure he'd ever be willing to walk away from China.

"Don't make any decisions about her without hearing what she has to say for herself. And that's if she's in the wrong. But if you're in the wrong, don't be a jackass, Smooth!"

"Why do you always have to make so much sense?" he asked Miranda.

"I've been where you are now. Maybe what hurt me is different than what's hurting you. I suppose it is too. But I had to make a choice just like you have to make one now."

"And what did you choose?" Smooth wanted to know.

"What was right for me," she stated matter-of-factly.

"Will you marry me?"

They both laughed hard.

"You got to divorce China first."

TWENTY TWO

The day after receiving Donna's name from China, Nick had everything else he needed. His information on her was limited to just a little more than the basics. It included her birthday, state I.D. information, work history, and credit report. But more importantly, his information contained an address—an address she had recently moved to.

After getting the address, Nick checked it out.

He parked his car and got out, carrying a small cake he'd purchased from a local bakery.

With the confidence of an A-list celebrity, he proceeded to the door. There was a car parked in the driveway, which startled Nick when the car started up. He was unable to get a clear view of the driver because of the dark-tinted windows, but he was fairly certain it was Monica.

He'd have to make sure.

He wanted to head back to his car and tail her, but he thought about how it would look if he abruptly turned around. Instead, he walked to the door and knocked.

"Who is it?" Donna asked, opening the door before receiving a reply.

She eyed the man in front of her suspiciously.

"Hi Ms. Kelly, my name is Kyle Spellers, and I'd just like to welcome you to the neighborhood," Nick pushed the box forward.

"Thank you so much," Donna replied, accepting the box.

"Would you like something to drink?" she asked him.

Seeing the invitation as a chance to look around the house, he gladly accepted.

"Yes, thank you."

"What would you like?" she asked, as she led the way to the large kitchen.

"Anything cold would be nice."

As Donna cut a slice of cake for him, Nick looked around for telltale signs of who all lived in the house.

Everything was extremely neat, but he did notice a variety of kids' cereals on top of the refrigerator.

Nick finished half of his cake and then looked at his watch.

"I have to excuse myself, Ms. Kelly. Thank you for your hospitality," he said, as he picked up his soda.

"Thank you for stopping by," Donna told him. She then walked him to door.

Before starting his car, Nick looked around at the street. He needed a place to park where he'd be able to observe the house. He drove away and then returned and parked in the driveway of the house next door, where he'd noticed a 'For Sale' sign. He settled in to wait for Monica's return. That's if, in fact, it was her. And if it wasn't, he was on the clock. China would pay for it.

Nick hadn't waited very long when the car he'd seen earlier returned to the house. He watched as all the car doors except the driver's side opened and out poured the kids. Finally, the driver's side door opened.

Nick picked up the ID photo that he had enlarged and was satisfied.

He found Monica.

* * *

Smooth picked up his phone to see who was calling so much. Seeing that it was China, he hit the ignore button and lowered his head back on the pillow.

His phone rang again. He checked the caller ID and was surprised to see China calling back.

"Yeah," he picked up.

"Hi, baby. How are you?"

"What do you want, China?"

"I got something to tell you that ..."

"I don't want to hear it!"

"You don't even know what I'm about to say."

"You're right," Smooth said. "I do know, though the last time you told me you had something to tell me, you flipped my world upside down, and you made me see for the first time that what I thought was love wasn't love at all."

Smooth's words hit China like a freight train and knocked her into silence.

She was silent, but he knew she was still on the line. He was glad to see the impact of his words.

"So you think all this time I didn't love you? That I don't love you?" China was angry now.

"I never doubted it before. Now I don't know what to think. You're to blame for that!"

"Are you trying to hurt me with your words?"

"No more than you tried to hurt me with your actions," Smooth retorted.

"I guess I deserve that."

"That and a lot more! What's the purpose of this call, China?"

China was devastated. Smooth had never treated her cruelly.

"You hate me, don't you?" she asked, even though she dreaded the answer.

This time it was Smooth who remained silent. He heard the agony in her voice and hated himself for what he was doing to her, but he wanted her to feel some of the pain he felt.

"Why did you call me?" he asked again, ignoring her question.

"If that's the way you want it, that's how it'll be. But let me make this clear to you, Smooth. I only did what I did because the only man that I'd give my life to looked like he was betraying me. I had pictures that told me he was betraying me. So I tried to turn the tables. Throughout it all, I still love you. You've cheated on me and I've forgiven you. I'm not going to beat a dead horse. I fucked up and I'm sorry, but I do love you." China gave her words time to sink in before she spoke again.

"Now to the reason I'm calling."

Smooth held the phone tightly. If China wasn't calling him to talk about them, her next words—the reason for the call—had to be important.

"I'm listening," he answered.

"I know where Monica is."

He wasn't sure he heard her correctly.

"What did you say?"

"I know where Monica is," she repeated.

Smooth closed his eye and said a silent prayer.

"You there?" China asked.

"Yeah, I'm here. Where is she?" he wanted to know.

"I'm not telling you."

"What do you mean you're not telling me?" he snapped. "You calling me to play games or something? Do you know where she is or not?"

"Nigga, I just told you I know. All I was about to say is I'm not telling you where she is unless you agree to work with me. China returned with an attitude of her own.

Smooth smiled on the other end of the line. He knew she would only take so much from him before she fought back.

"And if I don't agree?"

"I won't tell you where she is and I'll go after her myself."

"Why you going after her?"

Smooth regretted the question as soon as it was out of his mouth.

Still, he caught himself waiting to hear her answer.

"She got something that can hurt someone I love and I need it back."

Smooth smiled. China had said just what he'd hoped to hear. Just what he needed to hear.

"Okay," he told her. "We'll do this together."

* * *

Monica sat on the floor in her bedroom doing what she enjoyed most.

She never grew tired of counting the money or seeing the stacks she always made in front of her.

Without counting it, you'd never know that it wasn't the same amount she'd taken from China's closet. Minus the money for the down payment on the house and the investments she made, practically all of the money was still there. Monica had plans to dump large amounts into the up-and-comers she had recently researched.

Besides investing, she had no other plans for the money. She left her room and closed the door behind her.

"Aunt D," she called.

There was no answer. She looked in the kitchen and living room before pushing open Donna's bedroom door. She was lying in bed with the comforter up to her neck.

"Why are you opening my door without knocking?"

"Why are you still in bed?" Monica ignored Donna's question.

"I don't feel too good."

"So what am I supposed to eat?" she placed a hand on her hip.

"You can fix yourself something to eat, child. Close my door."

Monica walked out, leaving the door wide open.

In the kitchen she banged the pots and pans on the stove as loudly as she could. She regretted buying the house for her aunt. Maybe she didn't regret buying the house for her, but she definitely regretted moving in with her.

Monica thought her aunt was lazy. She didn't work, so what was the problem with cooking for her when she asked? Monica thought that it was the least she could do considering what she had done for her.

She set the stove to high and then placed the pan on the bright red element, just before she cracked an egg and dumped it in.

With no butter in the pan, she knew it wouldn't take long before the smoke detector went off.

She sat back and waited.

She hadn't waited long before the alarm brought Donna rushing in to see what was going on. The older lady snatched the pan off the stove, sat it in the sink, and then turned off the stove.

"What in God's name! Are you okay?"

Monica's only answer was the smirk on her face.

Donna looked at the young woman in front of her and wondered for the millionth time what happened to the sweet, loving girl that she was once proud to call her niece.

"You told me to fix my own food, didn't you?" Monica finally answered smartly.

Donna silently wished that she hadn't taken Monica up on the offer to buy her a house.

Donna felt trapped now with nowhere else to go. Since living under the same roof, she saw that Monica was extremely rude and disrespectful. She wanted to choke her.

"What would you like?" she asked instead.

"That's more like it."

Donna couldn't believe her ears. The disrespect was flagrant.

"Fix it yourself, you little nasty bitch!" she screamed, as she threw the cloth on the counter and attempted to walk out.

"You don't want to walk away from me," Monica held her by the arm.

Donna broke free and walked to her bedroom.

Monica had no intention of hurting her aunt in any way, but she needed to show her who was running things. She followed her to her room.

Donna had already placed several suitcases on her bed and began pulling things out of her drawers.

"What are you doing?" Monica laughed.

"You think you can disrespect me because you paid for this house? Child, you're nothing but a thief. The only real friend you ever had you don't have anymore because you stole her money. And now you just pushed away the only real family you have. You're in for a lovely life, little girl!"

"Where are you going to go?" Monica asked.

"I don't know, but I refuse to spend another day under the same roof with you!"

"So you're just going on the street?"

"No, unlike you, child, I have friends. But before I call on them, I'm going to ask you to give me some money."

"You're crazy!" Monica laughed.

"And you're evil. I wish you nothing but the best, child, but I want nothing to do with you anymore."

"Your choice, Monica turned around and walked out.

She knew that she was being a bitch lately, but she couldn't help herself. She was dealing with a lot and had no one to confide in. Couldn't her aunt see that she was stressed? She didn't want her to leave, but what was she supposed to do? Beg her to stay?"

That wouldn't happen.

Monica slammed the door to her bedroom. She went back to the piles of paper on the floor. That was all she needed.

TWENTY THREE

Smooth pulled up to Ga Ga's house and hit the horn. Instead of China, it was Roxy who came out to greet him.

She opened the door and sat in the passenger seat.

"What's up, Rox?"

"That's what I should be asking you."

"Why is that?"

"You and China good or what?" Roxy asked.

"We cool," was all he said.

"Where you taking her?"

"She's taking me somewhere. I'm just the driver."

Smooth didn't know it, but Roxy knew exactly where they were going. Not only where they were going, but what they were going to do.

"Smooth, I just want y'all to be careful. I can't say I wouldn't do the same thing if I was in your shoes. But I would make sure if I was to do anything like that, I didn't end up in your shoes. I know what y'all about to do. Please be careful."

Smooth only nodded, not confirming nor denying anything.

Roxy told him about how China kept her up all night talking about him.

Every now and then he smiled.

The two sat talking for a while before China finally emerged from the house.

"'bout time," Roxy said what Smooth was thinking.

"Whatever."

China got in as her sister stepped out.

"Hey Smooth," she said in greeting, as she closed the door.

"What's up? Where we headed?" he asked her.

"I didn't think of this before, but do you think it's a good idea for us to take your car?"

"What difference does it make?" he asked.

"Your car attracts attention and it's a car she knows pretty well."

Smooth agreed.

"We don't have much of a choice," he told her.

"Let me ask, Rox."

China got out and went back inside. A minute later, she came out dangling Roxy's keys.

Smooth locked up his car and made his way over to the other car.

China placed the tote bag she was carrying on the backseat and then got behind the wheel.

"What's in the bag?" Smooth asked.

"A few things I thought we'd need."

Smooth reached over and brought the bag to his lap.

He pulled out the outfit and looked at her skeptically.

She smiled.

After viewing the other items in the bag, he placed the bag back on the seat.

"What you got planned?"

Smooth listened as she explained her plan to him, which he believed would work.

"Where is she?"

"From what I learned from my P.I., she's staying at a house under Donna's name. I don't know if you remember her. They've only been living there for a week. I went by Donna's old place and it's empty, so I'm sure Donna and the kids are there. This time of day we can assume the kids are all at school."

Smooth nodded in agreement.

"Donna's probably there with her right now."

Smooth nodded again, understanding exactly what China was getting at.

"You still mad at me, Smooth?" she asked him.

"I don't know, China."

"You don't know if you're mad at me? How could you not know if ..."

Smooth shook his head. "I don't know if I was every mad at you."

"Hello, he pointed at her eye.

He leaned over and touched her eye.

"I did that out of hurt not anger. I didn't know how else to react to what you did to me."

"I'm not mad at you, Smooth. I deserved it. I hate that I messed up so bad with you."

Smooth fell quiet.

"Talk to me," China said, not liking the silence.

"Why didn't you think Monica stole your money?"

"Honestly, I didn't give anything or anybody a second thought once I saw those pictures. I was angry with you. I couldn't have been madder if those were pictures of you and Miranda in bed," she told him.

"But why?"

"Baby, how would you feel if you found out I cheated on you but you forgave me, and the only thing you asked is that I agree to stay away from the nigga I cheated on you with? But you get locked up and find out I went to see that nigga the same day you got locked up?" she waited for his response.

"I didn't go to see her the day you got locked up, but I understand everything you're saying."

Just then, Smooth started laughing.

"What's funny?"

"I don't know. I'm just thinking about all the days we talked about getting money and what we'd do once we got it. Neither one of us said any of this shit!"

"I know, right. I can tell you this though," China took one of Smooth's hands into her own. "If you give me another chance, I'll never doubt you again or put anyone or anything before you."

Smooth didn't pull back. He allowed her to hold his hand. He enjoyed her touch.

"I love you so much, Smooth. You got to believe that," she begged, with tears in her eyes.

"I do, China. I do," he replied, giving her hand a light squeeze.

"Good. Can I come home now?" she joked to lighten the mood.

"I never told you to leave in the first place. You didn't sleep at home last night?" he asked.

"That means you didn't either, nigga. Where did you sleep?"

Smooth was laughing before she asked the question.

"I'm just fucking with you, boo. I slept in our bed."

"Don't make me fuck you up, boy."

They both laughed.

"Once this is over, we got to go back," Smooth said.

"Back where?"

"To where we were before the money came."

"I'd like that," China told him.

"Okay, now it's time to focus on the job ahead."

* * *

Donna was in the living room taking down the photos she'd put up only a few days earlier, when the doorbell rang.

"Who is it?" she shouted, as she made her way to the door.

Before opening the door, she stole a look through the peep hole.

She opened the door to see the mailman going through his bag.

"Can I help you?" she asked him.

"Yeah, I got something her for Monica."

Smooth pulled out his gun and pointed it at Donna. He placed a finger over his lips while stepping over the threshold and closing the door behind him.

"Where is she?" he asked.

The lady pointed down the long hallway.

"Don't do nothing stupid, lady. My beef is with Monica, not with you," Smooth cautioned.

Donna nodded.

Smooth called China.

"Who else is here?" he asked, after hanging up.

"Nobody," Donna whispered.

"No kids?"

She shook her head.

Smooth directed Donna to have a seat. He sat where Monica

wouldn't see him if she came down the hall.

He noticed that the lady didn't seem troubled by his presence and he made a mental note to watch her closely.

He thought about shooting her right then, but he didn't want to give Monica the heads up and have her call the cops.

He heard the door open, so he hid his gun under one of the cushions from the couch, even though he knew it was China. He was playing it safe.

China stepped in and locked the door behind her. Her hair was wrapped in a ponytail and tucked under her baseball cap. The oversized jeans and football jersey concealed her identity well, but Donna immediately knew who she was.

"Hi China," Donna said, after only a glimpse of her after she locked the door.

Smooth picked up his gun again.

"Where is she?" China asked.

Donna pointed with her chin.

Smooth noticed that China was all business now, as she started for the hallway.

"Pssst," he called her back. "Let her call for her," he suggested.

Without a moment's hesitation, Donna yelled Monica's name.

There was no response.

Donna called again.

Smooth was feeling around the old lady. She was far too cooperative.

She called again without any prompting.

Just as China was about to walk down the hallway, she heard Monica's voice.

"What do you want? Why do you keep calling me?" she asked storming into the living room.

Monica's phone fell from her grip when she saw the two gunmen in the house.

"Hi Monica," China said to her ex-best friend.

Monica thought she heard China's voice, but how could that be? China was in jail.

China removed the cap from her head.

Monica gasped, as the tears started down her cheeks.

"Don't waste your time with the tears, boo boo."

Smooth noticed that Donna had a smile on her face.

"First things first," China spoke to Monica. "I don't hate you ... at least not enough to kill you. But I love Smooth enough to kill you to protect him. So either you tell me where it is or ... well, you know the rest."

"Please, China, I'm sorry. Please. I wanted to give it back to you. I'm so sorry. I'm sorry, China. Oh my God, I'm sorry!"

"I'm not here for the money. Now where is it? I'm not asking again."

What scared Monica more than anything was China's calmness.

"Promise me you won't hurt me."

"You're in no position to be making demands. Maybe you'll start talking if I shoot her," China turned the gun on Donna.

"Maybe I can tell you where it is," Donna said.

China raised an eyebrow.

"Do you even know what I'm looking for?"

"No, but if you tell me, I might know where it is."

"I'm looking for a gun," China told her.

"Come with me," she said, as she rose from her seat and headed for the back door.

"Go into the garage and bring the shovel with your, honey."

Smooth did as he was told and entered the garage cautiously. He retrieved the shovel and walked out the door behind Donna.

Monica watched in dread as Donna directed Smooth on where to dig. She felt the fear paralyzing her more and more, every time he thrust the tool forward. Smooth dug until he heard the metal of the shovel hit the box buried in the hole.

With the shovel next to him, he dropped to his knees and pulled out the box. The weight felt right. He shook off the excess dirt from it, and when he did, he heard the object shuffling around inside.

"Let's go back in the house."

Back inside, he placed the box on the table and opened it. The gun was wrapped in cloth, and Smooth quickly unwrapped it with trembling hands. The smile on his face after unwrapping the gun was all the verification China needed to know that he'd found the gun.

"How many bullets are in it, baby?" China asked.

"Check for yourself," he said, as he handed it to her and took the gun she was holding.

After checking, China put the clip back in and cambered a round.

"We already wasted enough time here," she turned the gun on Monica.

"Wait, wait, wait!" Monica screamed, holding her hands in front of her. "I'll take you to the money."

China shook her head.

"I didn't come for the money. I got what I came for."

Just as China was about to squeeze the trigger, she heard Smooth's voice.

"Where is the money?" he asked.

Monica turned to Smooth.

"I have it where it's safe."

China's anger overtook her. She drew back and struck the barrel of the gun across Monica's forehead.

She screamed out in pain as she fell to the ground.

China pounced on her and forced the gun into her mouth.

"Answer the question, bitch!"

China was so entranced with Monica and the hate that washed over her that she hadn't noticed that Smooth and Donna had walked away.

She hit Monica again and again.

"Where's the money?" she asked again.

China was still on top of Monica when Smooth walked back into the room carrying the suitcase.

"China," he yelled her name.

"Let's get out of here," he told her.

Slowly she rose to her feet.

Monica lay by her feet moaning in pain.

China looked down and fired four bullets into Monica's small rame.

Smooth noticed the smirk on Donna's face.

"What is it with you?" Smooth asked.

"Y'all just did the world a favor by getting rid of this filth!"

"Donna, I don't want to hurt you, but ..."

She silenced China.

"Baby, you don't have to worry about me. I was in the process of eaving her to herself anyway. I got to take care of the kids. I'm the only person they got left in this world."

A look passed between Smooth and China, and with that look they both agreed.

"How are you going to explain this?" China asked her.

"This is what I saw when I came back from my morning walk."

Smooth nodded. He opened the suitcase and took out several stacks and placed them on the table.

"Go get the car," he ordered China.

After returning, China turned to face Donna.

"Don't make me regret this."

"Hush your trap, child."

Smooth and China got in the car and drove away. They made it back to Ga Ga's without a single word passing between them.

Roxy was on the porch waiting when they arrived.

Smooth nodded indiscreetly to her. She returned his nod.

Now in Smooth's car, they headed home.

"Here," China said, handing over the gun with which she just killed Monica. The same gun he had killed Boss with months earlier.

"Why you giving it to me?" he asked her.

"So you can do something with it."

"What should I do with it?"

"Do whatever you want. I trust you."

Smooth smiled. "I trust you, too."

– THE END –

Text Good2Go at 42828 to receive
new release updates to your email.

You can write this author at
Jacob Spears #889544
A4-AC3
Martin County Jail
800 SE Monterey Rd
Stuart, FL 34994

Please support this author by
leaving your review. -Thank You-

To submit a manuscript for review, email
us at G2G@good2gopublishing.com

BOOKS BY GOOD2GO AUTHORS

GOOD 2 GO FILMS PRESENTS

To order books, please fill out the order form below:
To order films please go to www.good2gofilms.com

Name:_____

Address:_____

City:_____ State:_____ Zip Code:_____

Phone:_____

Email:_____

Method of Payment: Check   VISA   MASTERCARD

Credit Card#:_____

Name as it appears on card:_____

Signature:_____

Item Name	Price	Qty	Amount
48 Hours to Die – Silk White	$14.99		
Business Is Business – Silk White	$14.99		
Business Is Business 2 – Silk White	$14.99		
Flipping Numbers – Ernest Morris	$14.99		
Flipping Numbers 2 – Ernest Morris	$14.99		
He Loves Me, He Loves You Not - Mychea	$14.99		
He Loves Me, He Loves You Not 2 - Mychea	$14.99		
He Loves Me, He Loves You Not 3 - Mychea	$14.99		
He Loves Me, He Loves You Not 4 – Mychea	$14.99		
He Loves Me, He Loves You Not 5 – Mychea	$14.99		
Lost and Turned Out – Ernest Morris	$14.99		
Married To Da Streets – Silk White	$14.99		
My Besties – Asia Hill	$14.99		
My Besties 2 – Asia Hill	$14.99		
My Boyfriend's Wife - Mychea	$14.99		
Never Be The Same – Silk White	$14.99		
Stranded – Silk White	$14.99		
Slumped – Jason Brent	$14.99		
Tears of a Hustler - Silk White	$14.99		
Tears of a Hustler 2 - Silk White	$14.99		
Tears of a Hustler 3 - Silk White	$14.99		
Tears of a Hustler 4- Silk White	$14.99		
Tears of a Hustler 5 – Silk White	$14.99		
Tears of a Hustler 6 – Silk White	$14.99		
The Panty Ripper - Reality Way	$14.99		
The Panty Ripper 3 – Reality Way	$14.99		
The Teflon Queen – Silk White	$14.99		
The Teflon Queen 2 – Silk White	$14.99		
The Teflon Queen 3 – Silk White	$14.99		
The Teflon Queen 4 – Silk White	$14.99		
The Teflon Queen 5 – Silk White	$14.99		
Time Is Money - Silk White	$14.99		
Young Goonz – Reality Way	$14.99		
Subtotal:			
Tax:			
Shipping (Free) U.S. Media Mail:			
Total:			

Make Checks Payable To:
Good2Go Publishing
7311 W Glass Lane,
Laveen, AZ 85339

Acknowledgements

I want to thank Gvin for keeping me with new books, Zirger for a good laugh, Mary for keeping my head right & my Mom Lenora Sarantos. Last I would like to thank my brother Chris Hopkins.

To submit a manuscript for review, email us at
G2G@good2gopublishing.com

Epilogue

Smooth and China stood in the same spot at the edge of the lake where months earlier Smooth had thrown the gun that had killed two people. Before tossing the gun into the lake, he'd almost flattened the barrel with a sledgehammer. Even if the gun were retrieved from the lake someday, it would never be fired to conduct ballistic tests.

"Are you ready?" he asked her.

"As ready as I'll ever be," she replied.

They enjoyed the setting of the sun. It would be the last time they would be able to see it together for three years.

Mr. Hevralesky had arranged a plea deal that would send China to prison for three years.

She knew the severity of her charge, yet she was satisfied with the outcome. She was granted a two-week furlough and was scheduled to turn herself in the following morning.

"I spoke with Donna earlier today," she told Smooth.

"And?"

"The police have no leads or motives. They're saying it was a random act of violence."

Smooth shook his head.

"Are you going to give Roxy the money she needs?"

"That's your call, baby," said China.

"She got it then."

"She really loves you, you know that?"

"Yeah, I know. I love her, too. But not nearly as much as I love your crazy ass."

"You better not love nobody like you love me."

"I don't. Not even myself."

"Does this mean we're back or going back?" China asked him.